A Cheese of Some Importance

Mark R. Giesser

ISBN: 1508951799
ISBN 13: 9781508951797
Library of Congress Control Number: 2015904931
CreateSpace Independent Publishing Platform
North Charleston, South Carolina

PROLOGUE

All right, so I defied my parents.

I'm not the first son in the history of the world to do so. I just wanted to do something with my life other than follow the family business. It's not like I break into houses and steal the silver, or lure innocent girls into brothels, or dig up graves and peddle the contents to medical schools.

I gave up acting and became a clerk in the Patent Office.

Shocking, I know, and the cause of much palpitation and headshaking in theatrical troupes from Connecticut to Kentucky. Yet hardly a reason for divine justice to land me in the cellar of an abandoned tobacco warehouse, awaiting my murder.

But Dionysus, god of theatre, as my otherwise good Christian family will tell you, has a long memory and a unique sense of humor.

Which must be why I await my murder chained to a twelve-hundred-and-fifty-pound wheel of cheese.

Sheep's milk cheese.

I hate sheep.

I hate Andrew Jackson.

Well, I probably shouldn't hate him. I've never met him. And he is our great national hero, and might someday be president. Which means I'll essentially be working for him. Hating your boss makes for difficult days at work, and if there's one thing I do hate, it's that.

Assuming I live, which is doubtful. Maybe I should have shown more interest in my father's penchant for escape tricks. He always figured them for a crowd-pleaser when Hamlet dropped in the aisles like a dead pigeon. Too bad Mother was a purist. As long as she was the diva, the Lightner Company was absolutely not going to become a purveyor of cheap market-day entertainments. "Mixed marriages," Father would sigh as she confiscated his shackles. Although I always suspected she put them to good use on him after my sister and I had been put to bed. Which may account for my adult cravings for respectability. Which also may account for why I'm shivering in a dark cellar.

October in the District of Columbia. Last week it was still warm. As always, timing is everything.

Of course, sometimes you get lucky with timing. Back in January, General Jackson won the Battle of New Orleans after the peace treaty had been signed. Well, how was he to know? It's not like they can send paperwork across the Atlantic by balloon yet. Since we needed a great victory, the nation forgave the oversight in a burst of creative commemorative energy. But if the national mood had gone the other way the twelve-hundred-and-fifty-pound wheel of sheep's milk cheese wouldn't be here, and neither would I. So my predicament is Jackson's fault.

And Dr. Thornton's fault. Especially Dr. Thornton's fault.

If he wanted to find the damn cheese so badly, he should have gone after it himself. But no, the Superintendent of Patents is far too busy for legwork, let alone to put himself at personal risk. No, he has complete faith in the abilities of his chief clerk to rescue the great cheese and thereby rescue President Madison's administration from the gravest of political embarrassments. Or collapse.

I guess it does take a great cheese to topple a great man. Even if the president is only a little over five feet tall and scarcely a hundred pounds.

Thinking about that, it's just as well that he won't be giving me a medal. I've got eight or nine inches and about sixty pounds on him, and the newspaper artists would be tempted to make a cartoon out of the contrast.

Cartoon. Is that what future historians will make of this whole episode? Athenian democracy, the Roman Republic—at least it took Alexander and Caesar to destroy them. But for their American descendant to founder on account of a cheese? What does that say about the progress of mankind? And we seemed to be doing so well, too. Even if the British did burn Washington City last year, we still won the war. More or less. Well, we didn't lose. And the country held together despite bets taken to the contrary. So what will future historians say when the year 1815 sputters to a close with the hard-won American union split apart not over economic or cultural or religious differences, not even over slavery, but over the kidnapping of an overweight ceremonial cheese?

Listen to me. I'm beginning to sound like the minutes of the cabinet meeting that debated the ransom note. Not eating for the better part of two days clouds your thinking. Bodily humors out of balance, no doubt. Excess bile? Or would it be excess phlegm? Or to be strictly modern about it, am I simply experiencing what physicians now call a morbidly overstimulated state of bodily excitement? Having not had the chance lately to chart my bowels, it's hard to say. Whatever the reason, my stomach hurts. You'd think there'd be some leftover tobacco around here to take the edge off. I suppose I could sample the residue on the flagstones. But, then, I did promise Amanda I'd stop chewing and only take the occasional pipeful—and I don't have a pipe. Or a tinderbox with which to light one. Probably too damp in here to get a fire going anyway.

A little over a year ago that wouldn't have been a problem. The Brits were setting lots of fires, and, trapped in the Patent Office, Amanda and I came very close to being incinerated. That we pulled ourselves through was thanks in no small part to my acting skill and her skill at inventing an improved Congreve rocket. Impressed Dr. Thornton, which was no small feat. I think it even impressed her proper Royal Navy officer father, although the tone of his correspondence suggested otherwise. Shame she's not here to help this time. Excessively clever woman, my fiancée.

Just like my jailer. Along with some water, I've been left with a cheese knife. If I can't resist the urge to eat, I'm forced to violate the cheese and sully its value as a political symbol. So on the odd chance that I'm rescued before I'm killed, something's been achieved. A curious test of will. My dedication as a civil servant versus the primal instinct to survive. Spartan boy and wolf. Only far less heroic.

Dionysus has a unique sense of humor.

1

"You want me to find what, sir?"

"The cheese, Mr. Lightner. The giant wheel of cheese. The one that's been in the newspapers for weeks."

"That's been stolen."

"And is being held for ransom. That is the situation as I understand it. Do you wish me to repeat the assignment a third time, or can you grasp the idea from what I've explained so far?"

Frankly, I couldn't, but in the year and a half I'd been Dr. Thornton's chief clerk, I'd never been called into his private office simply to share a funny story. And the expression on his face didn't indicate that this time was the exception.

"Sir, isn't tracking down the cheese somewhat beyond the scope of this office?"

Dr. Thornton smiled slightly as he reached for the decanter of Madeira at the edge of his desk.

"Mr. Lightner, I'm pleased to see that my training has taken root. You've just asked the quintessential bureaucrat's question. The very question, in fact, posed to me earlier this morning by Secretary Dallas. To which I will provide the quintessential bureaucrat's manager's response: it is only this office that is capable of executing the task."

Treasury Secretary Dallas may still powder his hair and wear knee breeches, but he's a canny old Scotsman and not likely to have accepted that explanation at face value. Time to let Dr. Thornton expound. Somewhere in the tale there's bound to be a way out.

"Surely Mr. Dallas took exception to that," I said.

Dr. Thornton rose, wineglass in hand, and posed himself at the right side of the window behind his desk. A Gilbert Stuart moment in the making, if, indeed, there was a quick way of reaching Mr. Stuart and hurrying him over with his brushes.

"Not initially. After the ransom note was passed around the room, the cabinet agreed on two things. First, as the president is still relaxing himself at his Virginia estate, extra care should be taken to keep the matter from him as long as possible."

I'm not surprised. After years of internecine cabinet warfare, some calm prevails. The last thing anyone wants is to prime the president's tendency to see grand conspiracies, impose grand solutions like another damaging trade embargo, and start everyone sniping again.

"Secondly," Dr. Thornton said, "paying a ransom would necessarily involve a large public expenditure and inevitably reach the president's attention, thus violating precept number one. So someone had to find the cheese as quickly as possible."

Knowing the cabinet, passing the hat around the room wasn't even considered.

"Secretary Dallas then took the floor. He declared that as the cheese was not a foreign import subject to customs duties, and is a gift to the people of the United States rather than a purchase by the people, it was none of Treasury's concern. He suggested that since the cheese is intended to commemorate the upcoming anniversary of General Jackson's victory at New Orleans, the matter was War's responsibility."

"I can see where Mr. Crawford would have to agree."

"Mr. Crawford didn't. The secretary of war responded as if he'd been told one of his prize plantation studs had failed to perform. 'If the matter fell within the purview of the War Department,' he drawled, 'I'd have been at my desk drawing up military orders before the rest of you gentlemen had finished reading. I ask you, however, by what possible stretch of the imagination can the disappearance of a cheese be considered an incursion against the territorial sovereignty of these United States?'"

Dr. Thornton's imitation Georgia accent wasn't bad. I was tempted to suggest that if he ever tired of running the Patent Office, my parents could always use a middle-aged utility player. But I valued my employment.

"And that's when the question passed to you and Mr. Monroe?" I asked instead.

Dr. Thornton refilled his glass, then resumed his speaker's pose at the left side of the window. The afternoon sun highlighted the nap on his brown velvet coat better from that angle.

"No. At that point, Secretary Crawford declared that since the cheese spent a considerable portion of its journey from Vermont on navigable water, if any department should bear the burden of recovery, it was most assuredly Navy."

"Sounds reasonable."

"Not to Secretary Crowninshield. Which is understandable in view of the Navy Department's checkered history in managing its budget."

Dr. Thornton always takes pains to point out to Mr. Monroe how well we manage ours in contrast to other government offices. Of course, we don't have much to manage, but it's the principle that counts.

"I'm sure Ben Crowninshield didn't want to take on anything that might subject Navy to additional scrutiny," Dr. Thornton said. "So he told the secretary of war that there was no indication from naval dispatches that anything the size of the cheese had disappeared while on navigable water. And as no request had been made for any naval patrols of the Alexandria riverfront at the time the cheese was due in port, the Department of the Navy had no more responsibility than did the Department of War. In his view, the most appropriate official to investigate the matter was the postmaster general."

"Because of the large amount of postage due?" I asked. Dr. Thornton slowly turned his head in my direction, which was his signal challenging any attempt on my part at flippancy. Point made, I played innocent.

"Even at bulk rates, the shipping charges on a giant cheese from Vermont to Washington City would be a considerable sum to lay out up front," I said.

"That's if the postmaster at its point of origin had accepted the article in the first place," Dr. Thornton replied. "Apparently, because of confusion over applicable postal regulations, private freighting was arranged."

"So what was Mr. Crowninshield's point?"

"Simply that the postal department had responsibility for any ambiguity in its regulations that forced an American citizen to avail himself of private services and therefore deprived the Treasury of revenue. In effect, Postmaster General Meigs owed the nation in investigative work the lost value of the mailing."

Having studied some law prior to joining the Patent Office, I had to admire that argument most for its lawyer-like stretch of logic. However, the unamused postmaster general had persuaded Attorney General Rush to immediately render a contrary opinion. This finally landed the problem squarely in Mr. Monroe's lap. Dr. Thornton's dramatic instincts told him it was time to take a thoughtful pause and a slow sit.

"And thus the rescue of the great cheese devolved upon the secretary of state."

Which I guessed was the last thing that James Monroe wanted. Issues like the acquisition of Spanish Florida were on his mind, not to mention a probable accession to the presidency in next year's election. Even at twelve hundred and fifty pounds, a cheese from Vermont was not weighty enough to intrude. Yet no one else was left in the room to foist it on, and if Mr. Monroe wanted to look presidential, he couldn't very well not take charge. Even the shy, bookish President Madison could do that in a pinch.

"I tell you, Mr. Lightner, it's a good thing for the country that I was present at the meeting," Dr. Thornton said. "And to think that I had to remind the secretary of state about my having saved the government in order to present my budget request to the cabinet in the first place."

I noticed that I had been left out of that last remark, but I chalked that up to Dr. Thornton being in his official mode of thought. Stopping a squad of torch-happy British soldiers from burning the Patent Office building had been a team effort; at least, that's the way I, Amanda, Charlie Dunn, and Madeleine Serurier remember it. In his less guarded moments, Dr. Thornton will acknowledge that, but in the endless jockeying for federal money, he prefers to simplify things and leave us in the background. To his mind, there's a direct road from the city's destruction to his expansion: he saved the Patent Office when every other public building had been burnt to the ground, and so Congress had a place in which to reconvene. Which narrowly kept a grumpy Congress from moving the capital back to Philadelphia or New York, or, in total desperation, to Pittsburgh. Which allows those heavily invested in Potomac swampland a chance to get back their money. Which should mean that the cabinet gratefully unites to pressure Congress into giving the Patent Office more money. After months of correspondence, I suspect that Mr. Monroe granted Dr. Thornton a special audience with the cabinet because he figured that the other secretaries would all bear down on Dr. Thornton and shut him up. Too bad the ransom note arrived on the same morning.

"You do seem to have a knack for being where the country needs you most," I said. I didn't see the point of reminding him that he'd vacated the Patent Office as British troops crossed the city line and was only trapped there later by mistake.

Dr. Thornton took up his deliberative pose, folding his hands in front of him and resting his chin on his thumbs. "Mr. Lightner, were it not for your proven loyalty to this office, I'd think you consider this cheese business to be a trivial affair."

"Certainly not, sir. The patent application pending on the Brackenridge cheese press suggests a major industrial breakthrough. Clearly the absence of the commemorative cheese highlighting its efficacy deals the new process a severe blow."

Dr. Thornton eased back in his chair, satisfied by my clerk-like analysis. "But while that may affect a nascent cheese industry, or even raise the level of melancholia in Samuel Brackenridge's sheep, I must admit that I don't understand the larger national implications."

"In a word," Dr. Thornton said in a low voice—you never know who's hunched over a notebook in the alley below us—"secession."

Secession? Over a cheese? The worst summer heat and humidity were long past. The brains of our esteemed secretaries must have cooled by now.

"Secretary Monroe saw the threat with utmost clarity," Dr. Thornton continued. "After all, it was just last December that the rumblings in New England about leaving the Union reached the level of an actual convention. And with the South accusing New England of treason as a result, only General Jackson's victory and the peace treaty quieted things. The relative harmony at present may be an illusion, and an explosion could be triggered by the most unseemly incident."

"Like a gift cheese from New England disappearing in the South."

"Such disappearance being construed by New England as yet again Southern disregard for Northern sensibilities. And Westerners might decide that both sister regions had failed to protect a symbol of the honor of the West's great military hero. Fanned by rival newspapers, popular emotions could burn rapidly out of control. Street demonstrations, rock throwing, congressmen bashing each other with canes."

Dr. Thornton was working himself up for his "mobocracy" speech. I poured him another glass of Madeira to blunt the impulse. Personally, I didn't mind the idea of congressmen incapacitating each other, since wounded legislators are less apt to bother those of us charged with actually running the government. It was the thought of street demonstrators singing French protest ballads off-key that I found frightening.

"As Mr. Monroe laid out the scenario, I saw what was really on his mind," Dr. Thornton said. "Even if the president managed to keep the country intact, the damage to the Virginia dynasty might be irreparable. Mrs. Monroe's preliminary measurements for new White House draperies would be rendered meaningless. What's more, we would have to adjust to the supervision of a new secretary of state without Mr. Monroe's favorable influence."

Even more frightening. Unlike the great Republican mentor Mr. Jefferson, Mr. Monroe's interest in patent policy wasn't intense enough to bruise Dr. Thornton's toes. Budget wrangles aside, Mr. Monroe's continued term at State followed by eight years as president was good insurance.

"Suffice it to say that I stepped in to assist Mr. Monroe with his predicament," Dr. Thornton said. "Which brings me back to the secretary of the treasury's challenge. I submitted that the task of recovering the cheese is obviously a step in the final disposition of the Brackenridge patent, and since only this office has the expertise to deal in patent matters, it was up to us to recover it."

Us? Oh, of course. If I succeed, the good doctor claims a share of the credit, if not most of it. If I fail, well, good clerks are so hard to find these days. Hang on—maybe that was my way out.

"Sir, while I don't disagree with you," I said, "may I point out that one of the key reasons you've worked so hard to gain the cabinet's backing for your budget is our need for additional staff. If I'm out looking for the cheese, who's going to copy the documents, fill out the forms, process the fees and the filing, and run the messages?"

Dr. Thornton smiled again. "I expect this assignment not to impact your regular duties more than absolutely necessary. At any rate, when we recover the cheese, I should think that the cabinet will owe us enough personnel to rapidly overcome any logjam that occurs. And if not, volunteering extra hours to clear it can only enhance your annual evaluation."

Another quintessential bureaucrat's manager's response, about which further protest would have been futile.

"Good luck, Mr. Lightner. I trust you will be judicious with any expenses."

"Thank you, sir. I'll do my best."

"Don't forget to submit them on the Treasury's revised peacetime travel and entertainment forms."

"I won't, sir."

"And be discreet. The official government position is that the cheese is safely in storage awaiting its delivery for the January eighth celebration. Under no circumstances do we want any contrary news to go to the press."

I value my employment, but there are days when I wonder why.

2

"He wants you to find what?"

I was at my morning shopping in that rude and offal-redolent structure on Pennsylvania Avenue grandly dubbed the Central Market, doing my best to sift out a suitable picnic luncheon for later that afternoon. My English nature recoils at the notion of squandering a warm and bright Saturday in October, and I had no intention of doing so. Mr. Lightner, having found me picking over a rather dismal barrel of apples, was doing his best to explain why he had to postpone.

"A large cheese," he said. "A very large cheese."

To the relief of the corpulent farmer behind the barrel, I managed a third apple for my basket and handed over the required pennies. It was somewhat redder than green and relatively unblemished, which qualified it for inclusion more than less.

"These really should be for the cider press," I said to the farmer. His reply indicated a certain lack of regard for English expertise on the subject. I'd have engaged the man in further discourse, but Mr. Lightner seemed anxious to explain himself, so I motioned for him to follow me towards the bread stall at the end of the aisle.

"My Auntie Clarisse was a particularly good judge of apples, you know. Married a man from Dorset whose family wealth was founded on orchards, so I suppose she had to be. After all, in the course of a thirty-year marriage, one either learns something about the partner's inclinations, or ..."

"Amanda, I was talking about cheese."

"So you were. I believe there's some to be found at the third stall on the left."

"Why don't we stop and have a cup of tea? It'll be easier to talk."

"Cassius, we have the entire afternoon to talk. And a fair portion of the evening as well. The sooner I complete my marketing, the sooner we can converse. And anything else to which the food and wine lead."

Mr. Lightner frowned and looked around quickly to see if any of the nearby shoppers were listening. He's not particularly shy about sex, but he prefers that I not tease him about it in public places. Which is why I do.

"Unless you were planning on taking care of that on your own," I said.

"Amanda, do you mind?"

"What, discussing our physical needs? If you're uncomfortable with my doing so, perhaps you'd be best off back at Mrs. Woodley's. I understand that the House for Gentlemen of Creative Imagination is an excellent place in which to find big cheeses, day or night."

Mr. Lightner stomped away to inspect some turnips. I headed for the jellies at the adjacent stall, where one could easily forge an elaborate ceremony out of the inspection of a couple of simple crocks. After a properly frustrating several minutes, Mr. Lightner saw the jelly lady turn towards another patron, and abandoned the turnips.

"Why do you persist in thinking that I still patronize Mrs. Woodley's for those purposes?"

"Human nature? Men's nature, certainly."

"Don't turn this into a philosophical inquiry. The simple fact is that no matter how many times I offer an explanation, you refuse to accept it."

"Perhaps I just love the re-telling of a good story."

Mr. Lightner rolled his eyes. They're such a lovely emerald green that I never really mind the gesture.

"Where else am I supposed to see Anne?" he asked. "The office is hardly appropriate, and my boardinghouse less so. God knows the only reason my landlady tolerates your visits is because she's a secret admirer of the royal family."

"I have never claimed the slightest relation. What your landlady chooses to believe is hardly my responsibility. And why you still think you need to pay attention to Miss Frederick is a matter which you have not effectively clarified."

The jelly lady turned to us, her curiosity piqued. I opted for the crock of blackberry and walked on.

"Two things, Amanda. First, we're not married."

"I assure you, Cassius, as curious as some customs in this country are, I don't believe that visits to a boardinghouse constitute a sacrament."

"Secondly, just because I'm fond of Anne ..."

"You do keep using that word." I stopped at the pickles. As the pickle man was off chatting with the bread girl, it seemed as good a stall as any.

"How else would you like me to phrase it?" he said. "We're friends. We talk. It's not unheard of."

"We're friends. We talk."

"There's a difference."

"Which would be?"

Mr. Lightner fished a penny from his coat, slammed it on the board counter behind the pickle barrel, and proceeded to crunch a pickle. He'd chosen a large one, presumably in the hope that I'd move our conversation off that question by the time he finished. Which is why I didn't.

"Perhaps I misunderstand," I said. "You're referring to a difference in the tone of our voices. Or the cadences of our speech. Or is it that she furnishes you a receipt and I don't?"

"I have a cheese to find. Sorry about the picnic. I'll call on you when—well, if you want to see me, leave your card."

I gave him a decent interval then followed him out of the market and onto Pennsylvania Avenue. He was walking slowly, which he'd swear was to avoid tripping into a rut and breaking an ankle. He'd be partly right.

"Are we talking about the great Jacksonian cheese?" I asked.

"I thought we were talking about receipts."

"We were discussing cheese first. I'm sorry if we wandered off the subject."

"This is, of course, privileged information. Strictly."

"I shall report it only to the one or two known British agents on my list of social calls." Having elicited a smile, I took his hand in response as we picked our way down the road.

"In a nutshell, the cheese went missing sometime after it was offloaded at Alexandria," he said. "A ransom demand was presented to the cabinet."

"Indeed. A cheese-napping."

"That's the consensus."

"How very curious."

"People do steal things."

"Usually of some manageable dimension. Much past the size of your average hostage, it would seem an overly complicated business. Are they certain they haven't been hoaxed?"

"From what Dr. Thornton told me, a hoax wasn't even considered. They're all convinced we're on the brink of political disaster."

"Let me guess: a Northern gift disappears on a Southern wharf, leading to the mortification of a certain Western general. Embarrassment all around quickly changes into cross-accusation, insult, and some congressional heads having uncongenial introductions to some congressional walking sticks."

"At the least."

"I take it payment is not under consideration."

"You know the cabinet. Millions for defense, but not one penny for tribute."

"Not one penny out of someone's budget, anyway."

Finding ourselves suitably isolated, we paused at a large tree stump for a sit. Someday, Washington City may reach a level of sophistication sufficient to furnish public seating along its principal thoroughfares. At least the few poplars planted by Mr. Jefferson afford some shade. I adjusted my bonnet to remind Mr. Lightner of the care I'd taken to curl my hair the way he likes.

"Have an apple," I said.

"I'm really not hungry."

"If I'm going to be kissed, it will counteract the pickle."

One short apple and several lengthy kisses later it was clear that I hadn't changed his mind about the picnic. Unfortunately, I sensed that the quick diversion to his boardinghouse that would have done so was out of the question.

"It's a good thing I appreciate your conscientiousness," I said, retying my bonnet.

"Would you rather I was dismissed from the office and forced to leave the District?"

"I suppose I'm not in mind to break in a new clerk. Not just yet." I gave Mr. Lightner another kiss and nudged him onto his feet. "Do you have time to walk me back to my lodgings at the French Ministry?"

"Of course I do."

"Good. You can give these apples to Madeleine's cook whilst I change into my cheese-hunting frock. I imagine she can turn them into some form of tart that will pass muster with Minister Serurier."

"Amanda, this is government business."

"My gray plaid with the maroon stole should be sufficiently subdued."

"And it could be dangerous. If it's not a hoax, we don't know what sort of person we're dealing with. I could be facing a conspiracy employing a gang of thugs."

"Then I shall add my parasol with the sharpened point."

"Forget it. I'm taking you back to the ministry, where you can have a safe and relaxing weekend playing cards with Madeleine Serurier."

My instinct on the gray plaid was correct, but it did take the longest time to match it to the proper turban.

3

Too bad we couldn't advertise.

My first instinct was to place a notice in the *National Intelligencer.* "LOST: one giant wheel of cheese, last seen in the vicinity of the Alexandria docks. If sighted, do not attempt to remove, as such action may cause injury to the finder. Apply instead for reward to Dr. W. Thornton, the Patent Office (in the building formerly Blodgett's Hotel, within reasonable walk of the president's house)."

The stream of petitioners would at least keep the boss occupied while I figured out what in hell to do. And they'd probably leave the odd piece of cheddar as proof, padding my luncheon allowance. But I valued my job.

If this were London, as Amanda was happy to observe, we could seek advice from a professional thief-taker. Two constables patrol the entire District, neither man being what I'd deem an expert on doing so, let alone on any subtleties of the criminal mind. Which left me with a vague memory of a line from the old novel *Edgar Huntley,* where the hero, faced with a vexing mystery, resolves to make inquiries and to put interrogatories. It was the closest thing to a manual of investigative technique I had, and it seemed a more discreet method than staging a short play and hoping the kidnapper would reveal himself. Besides, most actors I know would refuse to be upstaged by a cheese.

Thus we found ourselves paying a call on Samuel Brackenridge, temporarily in residence at McKeowin's Pennsylvania Avenue hotel. His cheese, his cheese press, his pending patent. If he didn't have something I could work with, who would?

McKeowin's, a typical Washington City hotel of the Federalist brick townhouse variety, is neither particularly spacious nor elegantly appointed, and certainly not very private, but for a former diplomat, it was at least a respectable lodging. Respectable enough to have to argue my way out of an impolite challenge from the clerk manning the register, whom I didn't know, and who didn't realize we had a Patent Office. Well, in all fairness, if I really had been bringing Brackenridge my very pretty, well-shaped blonde companion for the afternoon, the clerk was entitled to his bribe. Just not on my budget.

"Now you see why it's better if you let me do this on my own," I said to Amanda as we walked upstairs.

"Nonsense. Whatever was he going to do to stop us, call a constable? Besides, it's strangely flattering to be thought attractive enough to command hard cash."

I was surprised that Brackenridge had settled for one of the smallest rooms under the third-floor roof. Sheep must be more costly to maintain than I thought. I spared him the expense of his offer of tea, at which he was relieved and Amanda was not.

"So Dr. Thornton has finally deigned to grant my patent," Brackenridge said. "I don't mind telling you, he has too much power, too much. The progress of American industry should not be held hostage to the whims of one man. But never mind that. One worry out of the way, at least. Very well, where's the document?"

Amanda and I exchanged glances. This wasn't going to be the most pleasant Saturday we'd spent.

"I'm afraid it's not quite ready," I said. I could see that Brackenridge was ready to teach me some new expletives in response, but he thought the better of it in Amanda's presence. I think she was disappointed. Instead, Brackenridge paced the room while he groped for an acceptable way to vent his anger. Not the most healthy thing for a man of his size and floridness to do, and for a man like that clearly into his forties, a sudden stopped heart is not unknown. I'm fairly close to that decade, so I try and stay as sanguine as I can. At least I'm in good physical shape, though I'll be damned if I can figure out where all my constant little aches and pains come from. Amanda says my imagination. I say it's good for our relationship that her admonishments are almost always made in the course of a therapeutic massage.

"But the good news, sir, is that I'm here to assist you," I said.

"With what?" Brackenridge snapped back. "I've already provided every possible piece of information your boss could want. For God's sake, man, it's only a new cheese press, not one of Robert Fulton's torpedoes."

The analogy was purposeful: though not necessarily authorized to do so, Dr. Thornton has a habit of delaying the grant of patents on inventions of interest to his pocket. He and the eminent Mr. Fulton had a legendary run-in. But that was quite before my time, and it is of interest to my pocket not to speak of any evil about which I hear. Dr. Thornton's kingdom, Dr. Thornton's rules, one less headache for Congress.

"Mr. Lightner has been delegated to find your lost cheese, and I am here to assist him," Amanda said curtly, stopping Brackenridge in mid-pace. He sat on the bed, breathing heavily. I poured him a glass of water from the pitcher on the nightstand, and he took several gulps.

"Did I hear you right, Mrs. ...?"

"Crofton. Yes, you most assuredly did."

"My apology for any offense, ma'am, but I can't say I'm pleased."

"Mr. Lightner is a particularly bright man of diverse talents, some of which need not concern you," Amanda said, lightly brushing the back of my coat at seat level. I frowned at her as she barreled on. "I am of the extended family of His Majesty's Navy, being both a frigate captain's daughter and a marine major's widow, and, having traveled extensively in two war zones, I am experienced in both the exploration of rough country and the construction of explosive projectiles.

I should think you doubly fortunate to have us involved in your predicament."

Brackenridge stared at us, his mouth open, still panting.

"Obviously, the cabinet considers the recovery of your cheese to be of top priority," I said. "The fact that you have a patent application pending on the new press in which the cheese was made means that it's not overly suspicious of me to ask after it, as opposed to an official from another department." Tenuous bureaucratic logic at best, but it was more diplomatic than telling Brackenridge that no other department wanted the job.

"The bastards won't pay, you mean," Brackenridge grunted. "Pardon my French, Mrs. Crofton."

"Oh, I never pardon the French, yours or anyone's," Amanda said in her best English deadpan. Brackenridge looked at her quizzically, then laughed.

"Mrs. Crofton, you remind me why, of all the diplomatic dinners I've endured, those hosted by the British were the most tolerable. Country at least has a goddamned sense of humor."

"You didn't like being a foreign minister, then?" Amanda asked.

"I didn't like the Balkans. Fried sheep guts and bitter coffee. I was only a consul, anyway, and frankly, the Ottomans are a decrepit bunch. Fine art and all that, but don't expect them to institute the vote anytime soon. Became somewhat partial to the cheese, though."

"And that's why you got into the business?" I asked.

Brackenridge, breathing easier, propped himself up on the bed pillows, took a plug of tobacco from the nightstand, and began to chew. I declined. Amanda reached into her reticule for her little enameled snuff box, put a pinch in each nostril, and sneezed delicately.

"Mr. Lightner, how long have you been a government clerk?"

"About a year and a half."

"About long enough to have your eye on another opportunity. At least you should. Just about anywhere you look in this country there's something you can make good money at. Good independent money."

Amanda smiled at me. "I've been telling him that since we met."

"Then you ought to listen to her," Brackenridge said. "A particularly bright man of diverse talents shouldn't bury himself under a pile of federal paper for too long."

"I'll keep that in mind, sir," I said.

"Take sheep. Around four years ago, I'm back on my farm in Vermont thinking that I ought to expand. Create some more wealth. But not just by snatching an acre here or there when my neighbors get fed up with breaking their plows on the granite and light out for the Ohio country. No, I figured domestic manufactures to be the future. And with the war hawks in Congress screaming for a fight with Britain, it wasn't too difficult to see that certain imported commodities would become as scarce as an old virgin in the Sultan's harem."

"Virgin wool, for example," Amanda said. "The sort that grows on sheep, not on young ladies." Brackenridge laughed again, and spat a stream of tobacco juice at the spittoon near the foot of the bed. At least they were having a pleasant Saturday.

"Mr. Lightner, you're lucky to have Mrs. Crofton for a lady friend. Not afraid to think like a man. Not easy to find in a woman."

"I thank you for the compliment," Amanda said.

Brackenridge obviously hadn't spent much time within earshot of a backstage women's dressing area, but I wasn't in the mood to enlighten him.

"Anyway, I imported a large herd of Merinos and a few books and started into the wool business. My neighbors thought I was crazy. I'll spare you my dog-training stories; suffice it to say that once I'd stumbled through the first winter, I had a big crop of good-quality wool ready to ship just as the war hawks finally got their war. And my neighbors? Once they saw our forces blunder around the Canadian border without getting a quick victory, they started searching out sheep auctions."

"Did they find any?" I asked. Maybe this all had to do with a jealous neighbor, although a Vermonter would hardly have an easy time organizing a cheese heist in the District of Columbia.

"Some did. Let's say since I had the guts to risk capital in an unproven market, I retained a certain advantage over latecomers," Brackenridge replied.

So envy was a possible motive, even if the logistics were prohibitive. Well, maybe we were getting somewhere. Maybe I could solve this sooner than later. Then again, *Edgar Huntley* was a thick book.

"As long as the war continued, and imports were blocked, anyone who got their hands on a sheep or two prospered," Brackenridge said.

"Or at least enjoyed themselves," Amanda said. With this round of chuckles, Brackenridge almost swallowed his chaw. I eased myself between Amanda and the bed.

"Of course, when Mr. Madison signed the peace treaty back in February, I got to thinking about economies of scale. To compete with British wool would take a whole lot more sheep, but now the Brits had the certain advantage, and I might not be able to keep up. My neighbors are crafty Yankees, and though they might be more conservative than I, they saw the problem, too. Most scrambled to sell the few animals they had for hides and meat. But hides and meat are worth less than wool, and it seemed a shame to slaughter a nice herd of Merinos."

"Killing does have a finality about it," I said. Brackenridge just nodded. Father always said sex was funnier than death, but you work with the opening you have.

"So then I got to thinking about another certain advantage I had, and that was the cheese I took a shine to in the Balkans. Kashkaval, they call it. Made from sheep's milk. You know it, Mrs. Crofton?"

"I believe I sampled some a number of years ago, when I visited my father on station at Malta. If I remember correctly, it has a taste and consistency not unlike cheddar."

"Very much so. Now, in America, cheese *is* cheddar, right? If I could start a taste for cheddar made from sheep's milk, and here I sit with that fine herd of Merinos, well then, there's one part of that certain advantage."

"And the other is the cheese press?" I asked.

"Economy of scale. Farms make cheddar if the lady of the farm is any good at it, but not everyone's good at it, and a family farm's a family farm. Not much export potential. A cheese press that simplifies the process speeds it up. Speed it up, you've got volume, volume gives you export potential."

"And export potential gives you an industry," Amanda said.

"And the patent gives you a head start on the market," I said. Brackenridge grinned and spat.

"You two ought to think about investing," he said. "Still time to join me on the ground floor."

"I'll keep that in mind, sir," I said, and nudged Amanda's foot as she began to speak. She pretended to clear her throat and kept quiet, but I knew I'd hear about it later.

"Mr. Brackenridge, what's the current situation with your neighbors?" I asked. "Are they scrambling to buy more sheep?"

"Not so far. Haven't met a Yankee that relishes getting burned in a business deal more than once. Besides, they can all understand supplying an existing need, but not too many can see how to create a demand for a product that's not yet established."

"Still, you've taken pains to keep the specific nature of the cheese secret. That would indicate that you harbor concerns about them jumping in behind you."

"Always prudent to keep everyone guessing. That's an advantage over the minister who organized the giant cheddar for Mr. Jefferson back in '02. No mystery about that one. And as you've seen since the cheese left Vermont, the newspapers love the mystery."

Secrecy feeds the imagination, though, and imaginations love to gallop. Someone resentful of Brackenridge's survival skills sits down over an ale or two with someone else who suddenly realizes he's been shortchanged on a meat-and-hides fire sale. An earlier generation in New England might have deemed Brackenridge a witch, and hanged him. What would our more enlightened generation do now to level Brackenridge out?

"Mr. Brackenridge, I'm no expert on dairying. But I don't see how you managed to mass milk a herd of sheep without anyone boasting about it."

"Money, I would imagine," Amanda said, tight-lipped.

"Got it in one, Mrs. Crofton. Hard cash isn't the easiest commodity to come by in my county, or most anyone else's. Especially for the average farmhand."

"Average farmhands get drunk," I said.

"They do. And they get laughed at for spitting out tall tales about milking a few hundred sheep in a day. It's just not something Vermonters are used to hearing, and what they're not used to hearing, they don't tend to believe."

"Which allows you yet another advantage in the race to market," Amanda said.

Brackenridge reached past me to pat Amanda's hand. "Mrs. Crofton, did you say you were interested in investing? I have to tell you, a woman with your head could do very well in the cheese business."

"Assuming you have a cheese business," I said.

"Oh, I'll have one, Mr. Chief Clerk. One way or another."

Which suggested that he had a plan B in the event I didn't find the cheese. What that suggested, I hadn't a clue. But I bet Edgar Huntley wouldn't have, either.

4

"Cassius, the man is quite my senior and spits far more tobacco than I find amusing."

"But you do find his business prospects alluring."

"Of interest, certainly. As should you."

To which my normally attentive Mr. Lightner's response was to bite harder into his bread and cheddar, and continue to study the effect of candlelight on the color of claret. Supper in his room following our meeting with Samuel Brackenridge was not proceeding as an unalloyed pleasure.

"You really should have a slice of ham with that," I said. "I splurged. Top-class Virginia."

He waived it away. "Maybe if you splurged less, you wouldn't be constantly on the lookout for investment schemes."

"Pardon?"

"I'm the first one to admit that I do not draw an overly generous salary."

Generous and salary cannot, in the rules of polite grammar, be accommodated in the same sentence when speaking of a federal clerkship, but I restrained myself from pointing that out.

"However, I am capable of advancement," he added.

At present, not without murdering Dr. Thornton, which, although some inventors would consider that a favor, was probably not advisable.

"I never said you weren't." I started on the ham.

"After all, I could have just stayed with my family and inherited the acting company."

"I have always commended you on your lack of tolerance for rotten fruit."

He poured himself more claret, drank, and continued looking into the glass. I mimicked his stare, hoping to provoke a smile. I didn't. Nonetheless, ever since my husband's exaggerated sense of honor got him skewered to death in an insignificant skirmish in an insignificant part of Spain, I tread carefully around the male mind.

"Cassius, if I didn't have complete faith in your ability to take care of us in future, I wouldn't be sitting here. It's just that, well, like Mr. Brackenridge said, this country is brimming with possibility. I see no reason why you should be averse to it."

"In the future."

"Tomorrow is Sunday. I should think the opening of business week on Monday would do nicely." Still no smile. I could feel myself losing patience with the intricacies of cross-cultural romance.

"You know," I said softly, "when we find the cheese, you're bound to get some sort of commendation. I bet that will open a door or two."

"Was that the royal 'we' or was I being included?"

"Oh, that's enough! If I'm to spend the remainder of the evening playing games, I'd rather do so at the French Ministry. Madame Serurier cheats, but she doesn't sulk."

Mr. Lightner caught me by my shoulders as I opened the door. My maroon stole does take some time to drape.

"It's too late for you to walk back on your own."

"You may escort me if you like, but only if you remain out of conversational range."

"I don't know. My feet are suddenly quite sore. If I limped too far behind, who knows what might happen to you."

"No telling how many cats might sniff out the subtle residue of ham on my fingers and follow me home."

"Didn't you once tell me that ham residue makes an excellent remedy for foot pain?"

"I doubt it. But experimentation is the key to progress."

Which indeed it was. And no doubt we'd have spent the whole night pleasantly wrapped up together under his quilt had it not been for the crash of barrels and the cry of pain that woke us around three.

❧

"I don't think anything's broken, but I'd advise a few days of bed rest to be certain."

A steaming pot of breakfast tea is one of the things I enjoy waking up to on a chilly Sunday; bandaging the ankle of a scruffy young man named Walter Clarkson was not. And if he hadn't been an acquaintance of Mr. Lightner's, I'd have insisted on giving him to one of the District constables, *sans* repair. That, however, would have necessitated finding a constable, and I was hoping to salvage some of our weekend. As it was, Mr. Lightner had to improvise a story for his landlady about why his perfectly sober friend chose an uncivilized hour to visit. I assured her the Prince Regent had similar experiences, and she groggily made her way back to bed upon promise of hearing them, shooing the other residents into their rooms.

"You're a very talented *fille de joie*," Clarkson said. Had I heard him correctly? "Though a man in your position has to be careful, Cass. How do you know this fine *fille* isn't spying for the Brits, or worse, our supposed friends, the French?"

He may have been attempting joviality, but as I wasn't sure, I twisted the last of the bandages in the wrong direction. He howled.

"Walter, you really don't want Mrs. Jenner to come back with an axe handle, do you?" Mr. Lightner said as he grabbed Clarkson's chin. Clarkson grunted an unclear response, which we interpreted in the affirmative. "Good. Then keep your mouth shut and apologize to Mrs. Crofton."

I didn't think it was worth pointing out the contradiction.

"I was trying to be nice," Clarkson said.

"So was I," I said. "Had I twisted ten degrees more to the left, I'd have shattered the bone."

Mr. Lightner poured the remnants of the claret into two glasses, handing me one. Clarkson reached eagerly for the other.

"I don't believe I heard the word 'sorry,' or the phrase, 'I was a rude idiot,' did you, Amanda?" Mr. Lightner said.

"Not that I recall. Of course, if Mr. Clarkson's French functions at the level of sophistication indicated by his behavior, he could have been attempting to call me a nurse rather than a prostitute."

"Is that what you were doing, Walter?"

"No, it wasn't. But I'm dying to hear the alternate explanation."

"Then I'll assume the word you were groping for is 'fiancée,'" I said. Clarkson took a moment to digest this. "It's a simple alternative which might have occurred to you were it not, perhaps, beyond the scope of your comprehension."

"I think Walter understands the concept, Amanda. It's just not something that a man who aspires to be one of Mrs. Woodley's regulars likes to think about."

So that's where they knew each other from. I shot Mr. Lightner a nasty look, making him decidedly uncomfortable.

"I don't get over there too often," Clarkson said. "We really only know each other from Frenchy Nordin's." He had a decent streak after all, even if I wasn't quite ready to believe that he and Mr. Lightner were only tavern friends.

"Well, I suppose that would also explain why we've not previously met," I said. Mr. Lightner looked relieved.

"Cass never mentioned that he was engaged."

"It's not exactly like we drink together on a regular basis."

"Not to worry, my love," I said, giving Mr. Lightner a peck on the cheek. "An occasional lapse of memory can be forgiven until we're married."

Clarkson did his best to suppress a burst of laughter. Frenchy Nordin's customers wouldn't once Clarkson was well enough to stumble back in.

"Anyway, please accept my apologies for jumping to conclusions, Mrs. Crofton."

"Accepted." Clarkson got his claret and took several sips without saying anything further.

"All right, Walter," Mr. Lightner said, "any particular reason you were lurking around the back of my boardinghouse?"

"Come on, Cass. You know how easy it is to get lost around here on a dark night. Even carrying a lantern."

"Walter, you wouldn't normally carry a lantern either to Frenchy's or Mrs. Woodley's, and you're not known for carrying one in your sleep. I'd have to guess you were on an open-field hike between neighborhoods. Why?"

"Not bad, Cass, not bad. Maybe you ought to consider leaving the Patent Office and becoming a federal marshal."

"Amanda, would you care to check the bandages on Mr. Clarkson's ankle? They look a little loose to me."

"Oh, dear. I do so take pride in my nursing skills," I said, and toyed with the perfectly tied slipknot until Clarkson yelled.

"Okay, okay! I was rummaging through the garbage. And you might warn your landlady about those big tree roots. I'm not so sure I won't sue."

"Mrs. Jenner would have no qualms about getting a writ of trespass drawn against you in response," Mr. Lightner said. "In fact, she might be persuaded to do so first, and I might be persuaded to change that story I concocted and help her."

If only. I keep thinking that if I ultimately can't interest him in a viable business venture, I might be able to persuade Mr. Lightner to reconsider applying for admission to the bar. But that's another matter.

"For free, of course," Mr. Lightner added. "Acting merely as a concerned tenant and friend of the court. And if I'm involved, you know Dr. Thornton would have to put in his two cents. At which I'm sure Joe Gales could find space in the *Intelligencer* for a few paragraphs. Yes, I think a lawsuit might be just the thing. Definitely get your name in the paper, though not exactly as an editorial staff credit."

A would-be Fleet Street hack. I went to the basin and pitcher to rinse my hands.

"Well," Clarkson said, drawling the word like a general-store draughts player, "I might lean towards considering the tree an occupational hazard. Of course, some information might nudge me in that direction."

"About what?" Mr. Lightner said. And then it struck me: no one of any prominence lives in Mr. Lightner's boardinghouse. And since newspaper filler is not usually worth the risk of broken bones ...

"Cheese," Clarkson said. "Twelve hundred and fifty pounds of it."

I nearly dropped the pitcher.

"You went to all this trouble to have me read you old newspapers?" Mr. Lightner said.

"Cass, if your boss wasn't such a fanatic about fresh air, he might find it easier to keep his instructions confidential."

"Walter, if you spent less time crawling in alleys, maybe Joe Gales would pay attention to your submissions!"

"He can get all the dinner party gossip he wants himself. Where else should I sniff around for something to impress him?"

Mr. Lightner eyed the fireplace poker. I tapped his shoulder and shook my head.

"How'd you know to be behind the Patent Office on Friday afternoon?" he asked Clarkson.

"Some chance, some deduction. I was walking near the Octagon House and saw a man in a powdered wig and breeches go inside. Didn't see his face, but who else dresses like that but our esteemed secretary of the treasury? Since the president's in Virginia, I wondered what brought Mr. Dallas to the Octagon, and figured it was worth a lookout. As the rest of the cabinet showed up, I knew I'd stumbled onto something, so when Dr. Thornton came hurrying out later, I decided to follow him back for a listen."

"Who else have you told?"

"Cass, I think the question is more who else could I tell?"

"Do you realize how serious this matter is?"

"What, the country's going to split up over a missing cheese? Yeah, yeah, I heard enough of the Doctor's theory. Reminded me of that overblown speech he supposedly used to keep the Brits from burning his precious office."

A team effort which included two ladies, but only the ranking gentleman gets the credit. So much for the judgment of history working out with any semblance of justice.

"Walter, you might dismiss Dr. Thornton's rhetorical style, but not his intellect, and not his instincts. The speech worked, didn't it?"

"I wasn't a witness. Could've been the Brits were getting tired and their torches were burning out."

"A properly prepared British torch does not burn out prematurely," I said. "Unlike their American counterparts."

"I'll bet Cass is the exception."

I frowned at Clarkson but he simply smiled back.

"Walter, get out of here," Mr. Lightner said.

"I'm an injured man. I need bed rest."

"Tough." Mr. Lightner hauled Clarkson to his feet and dragged him towards the door. After enjoying a few of Clarkson's squeals, I blocked their exit.

"Best not to re-awaken the house," I said.

Mr. Lightner stared me down for a moment, then deposited Clarkson onto one of the dining chairs. He then plopped himself in his wing chair and slammed his legs onto the accompanying footstool. I pulled the footstool away and perched on it. Clarkson glowered at us, rubbing his ankle.

"If anything's broken now, I will sue. I'll swear out a criminal complaint as well."

"Cassius, I distinctly recall telling Mr. Clarkson to watch his step as he left the room against my advice."

"So you did. To which I'm sure I added something about the tricky nature of that staircase, even under lantern light."

"Fine," Clarkson said. "But don't think for a minute that I'm backing off, even if I have to work my way around town on crutches.

Exposing a conspiracy of silence by the entire cabinet? Joe Gales'd give me a partnership for that."

Mr. Lightner responded with the eloquent bluntness of ancient Anglo-Saxon, which, having eavesdropped on many seamen in my girlhood, only offends me when unimaginatively overworked. That dampened the conversation into the sullenness of a little-boy tiff, so I resigned myself to solitaire until sunrise allowed Clarkson to leave in some safety. Which still might have allowed us a decent Sunday had it not been for the messenger from the city jail.

5

Unlike some actors who play Othello, my father used only a touch of burnt cork on his face, figuring that the power of suggestion would darken his complexion to the satisfaction of the audience. It saved money on makeup, but also impressed on me the lesson that it's easy to see someone for what he isn't when circumstances prime us to do so. Thus my shock upon reading a note from Charlie Dunn that he was jailed as a runaway slave. Last year, when we saved the Patent Office, Charlie was white.

Wasn't he?

"You're still staring, Mr. Horn Player. Maybe you'd best be asking the deputy marshal for another candle so you can figure out what it is you're looking at."

What I was looking at was the same broad-shouldered, dark-haired, plain-faced sailor I remembered. Who still remembered me as a bandsman with the District militia. Propped up on his bunk against the back wall of the cell, I could swear that he hadn't changed, except for a little extra dirt on his face. And jails are hardly places in which to keep scrubbed. Certainly it was the same deep voice, talking in the same accent that suggested an upbringing somewhere between northern Maryland and upstate New York with a reasonable amount of schooling. Definitely not the speech of a Virginia field hand.

But then the Moor spoke well enough to win the favor of a Venetian aristocrat's daughter.

"You did tell the deputy that they'd made a mistake," I said. I realized how stupid I sounded, but it was the best my addled logic could muster.

"I suppose I could have," Charlie said. "And there was some debate to that effect between him and the jailer. But the navy taught me not to lie, and it seems to have stuck."

I still didn't comprehend the reality in front of me. Not that I have anything against free blacks. My family and I met a fair number in our travels—possibly because free blacks and actors tend to rate at the same unelevated social level—and they seemed as decent a sort as any. Slaves are another story entirely, the poor souls. I can't see any excuse for allowing them, although I admit I don't understand anything about the economics of running a plantation. And if a man as urbane as Dr. Thornton keeps a slave, well …

No. It's not right. In fact, it's damn evil. I know that, and I think Dr. Thornton does, too. However, the law is what it is. And if it decides that Charlie's a runaway, no amount of moralizing is going to keep him out of trouble.

"I guess when we were out testing Amanda's rocket against the torching squad, I didn't notice," I said.

"Color's not usually a problem when two guys have to cover each other's asses in a fight. Though I don't recollect anyone in the Patent Office making any hash out of my appearance that day. And there sure was enough firelight to judge by."

"We all had other things on our minds."

"And anyway, I'm in that awkward band of coloration. When I was on cruise in the Mediterranean, the locals often thought I was from Naples. They heard the name Dunn, thought, okay, Papa was an Irish sailor, Mama was the woman in port. How I got aboard a United States frigate was my business. Not that they had anything against free men of color—so they said—but the Neapolitan me did get treated to more wine. So I can understand why even a well-meaning gentleman like yourself would be confused."

"Was Papa an Irish sailor?"

"Good a story as any."

Charlie puffed on his pipe while I digested all this. During our first encounter he didn't seem particularly the patient sort. Not unlike Amanda, which may account for why they took an instant dislike to each other. Now at the time, she was an enemy alien and he did hold her at gunpoint, so there was bound to be some friction. He earned her respect, though, and she his, and the concern she voiced for him when I was required to leave her in the front room of the jail was genuine.

"Well, Mr. Horn Player, have your eyes adjusted yet?"

"Pretty much."

"Hope that doesn't change things with us, but I expect it might have to."

"I'm still here to help."

"Of course you are. You're from the government, ain't you?" Charlie and I chuckled, and I felt a little less tense.

"We could start with why they arrested you," I said.

"I could answer that with a long, salty yarn, but let me see, you and that English lady—Mrs. Crofton—you still together?"

"Quite regularly. We're engaged. More or less."

"Which usually means less."

"What's that got to do with your arrest?"

"It's got to do with the length of my explanation. If you're more or less engaged, she ain't likely to let go of you for too long on a Sunday. So I'd best give you the short version: whiskey, women, whack on head."

"Your head or someone else's?"

"Both."

"Common enough. Why didn't they just turn you in at the Navy Yard?"

Charlie drew a few more puffs before answering. "I've been decommissioned."

Mr. Jefferson's gunboats. Conceived long before the war as a cheap way out of building a real blue-water navy, and worth about every penny not spent on them. Unstable, easy to sink, low on firepower, quick to rot. Finally scrapped. But men like Charlie who'd volunteered to serve on them shouldn't have been, even in peacetime. Surely the newer frigates needed experienced master gunners.

Maybe not if they were black.

"Well, I should say I resigned," Charlie said. "Didn't much want to take a demotion to get a new berth, especially after it became clear that my color no longer matched those of a warrant officer, and wouldn't anymore be likely to. Twenty years up from cabin boy, and that's what's offered. I have to tell you, I ain't felt right since."

"No chance on a merchant ship?"

"Not really the same. Truth is, I liked my guns, and I liked the idea of defending the country. But don't you ask me the hell why."

"I won't. I am sorry the navy did that to you. For what my opinion's worth, it wasn't right."

"Right now, your opinion may be what I've got to keep off the auction block."

"A simple drunken revel by an ex-sailor shouldn't go down too badly with a magistrate. Tell me where to get your discharge papers so I can get the deputy to change the booking on your arrest."

When Charlie again failed to answer right away, I knew that freeing him wasn't going to be that simple.

"Couple of things on that, Mr. Horn Player. First, I've only been picking up some casual labor, and the money's always asked to be spent on entertainment before shelter. Very persuasive, those coins are. So I ain't exactly had what you'd call a fixed place of residence for some time. Second, I didn't have the papers on me when I woke up in Mrs. Woodley's back room, which was about the time one furious city marshal told her to have her boys haul me over here."

"You got into Mrs. Woodley's?"

"The Neapolitan me did. Yesterday was three months since my discharge. Had some pay, which figured for once that I deserved something better scented than the waterfront girls. I spruced up as best I could, and introduced myself at the door with a few Italian words and a bunch of big gestures. Mrs. Woodley had to look hard at me more than once. Couldn't seem to make up her mind, which is when I guessed she might know you, so I said I was a friend. Didn't think you'd mind particularly."

"No. I suppose I'd have played along if I'd been there."

"So there I was. My brain had done about all the work it wanted to for the night. In fact, once I started on some of her best bourbon, it stopped thinking and got stuck on a song about a donkey. Or a hat. Or maybe a donkey in a hat. Or doing something to a hat. Which kept wanting to be sung out louder and ruder. I seem to remember it going over good that way with the girls in Naples. For some reason, Mrs. Woodley's ladies didn't take to it."

"Which got you the whack on the head."

"Took out her best boy first."

"And the city marshal happened to be upstairs."

"At one of those moments you don't want to be distracted."

Timing is everything.

"You think he had your papers misplaced?" I asked.

"Wouldn't be surprised. Wouldn't bet too hard on getting them found, either."

"I'll get over to the Yard tomorrow and start someone working on replacements."

"Likely to be chopping Maryland tobacco long before the navy gets around to it."

"Maybe I can get Dr. Thornton to intervene."

"Pitting him against the city marshal and Mrs. Woodley? Likely to be chopping Louisiana sugarcane by the time that's settled."

We were both stuck for an answer when Amanda walked in.

"Hello, Mr. Dunn. I'd say you were looking well, but I don't imagine you're in the mood for idle flattery."

Charlie grinned and shook hands with Amanda through the bars of the cell.

"Good to see you again, Mrs. Crofton. Though I'd have preferred a better reception hall."

Amanda turned to me as I was about to speak. "Yes, I decided it was time to pay off the jailer. No, it didn't require more than some pin money and a pinch of my snuff," she said, turning back to Charlie. "I hope you don't mind that I deemed his price for an escape to be out of the question."

"I'd have been jealous, anyway," Charlie said, which made Amanda smile for the first time in several hours.

"Amanda, there's something you need to know about Charlie," I said.

"Is it something absolutely horrid?"

"No, but …"

"Mr. Dunn, you haven't developed a penchant for eating snails, have you?"

"Not even when I was in Marseille."

"Oh, well that's all right, then. We can deal with anything short of that."

"Charlie's black," I said.

"I'd have thought that was obvious," Amanda said.

"I didn't think so."

"Cassius, I told you the charge wasn't mistaken on account of Mr. Dunn's color. Honestly, Mr. Dunn, you'd have thought I was speaking Sanskrit."

"How did you know he wasn't, say, Neapolitan?"

"Because I have been to Naples, which you have not," Amanda said.

"And I've done two farces by Goldoni, which you have not!"

Charlie stretched out on his bunk. "If you two are about to have a long and pointless fight, why don't you take it out front and wake me when you're finished."

Amanda took a deep breath. "Cassius, have you figured out how to secure Mr. Dunn's release?"

"Not quite."

"Would you tell me how you see the problem?"

I explained how Charlie wound up out of the navy and in the cell.

"You are, of course, far more the expert than I, but as I understand the law, what's needed is for a white man to provide evidence of

Mr. Dunn's free status and pay the costs of his imprisonment. Is that correct?"

"It is. A night's jailing I can provide. The evidence I can't."

"Why not? You can swear as to his conduct last year at the Patent Office. So can Dr. Thornton."

"All we can swear to is that we spent time with a man we thought was white—at least I did—who said he was a master gunner on a U.S. Navy gunboat."

"Don't forget the sailor suit," Charlie said.

"The city marshal will say one, how do we know he wasn't lying, and thus two, how do we know he didn't steal the suit off a dead sailor? No, without some papers, I think we're stuck."

"Then we'll have to provide some," Amanda said.

"I already told you why the navy bureaucracy's a dead end."

"Then we shall find a bureaucracy which isn't. Mr. Dunn, you look like a man in need of new employment. What else have you done besides blow people out of the water?"

"Last seen shifting cargo on the Alexandria docks," Charlie said.

"Indeed," Amanda said, smiling at me. "What an excellent recommendation."

So it was that Dr. Thornton anticipated the gratitude of the cabinet and hired Charlie as Patent Office messenger. Three months ago. I must admit, Amanda's a much better forger than I am. Someday, she will make a wonderful wife.

And if we were lucky, we'd find the cheese before the city marshal bothered to find Dr. Thornton.

6

Deep purple really is not my color.

That is to say, heavy deep purple draperies trimmed in chartreuse fringe framing windows surrounded by periwinkle-patterned wallpaper. With my reflection bouncing around all those gold-framed mirrors, I was forced to conclude that dressing seasonably in russet was not the most harmonious choice I could have made. Well, Madame Serurier's forest green didn't seem quite right, either, and if anyone would have known how to coordinate, it would have been her.

Anyone respectable, that is.

"My first time in a whorehouse and I guess incorrectly," she said as we sipped our coffee. "I should have come right out and asked Louis."

And if she had, I imagine that Minister Serurier would have answered forthrightly, but there are some things between husband and wife that even the French don't do.

"A tasteful silver service, though, do you not think?" she said. "Parisian, surely."

"The pieces could be locally made copies."

Madame picked up the coffeepot and examined its bottom. "A Parisian hallmark. Not the best, but reasonable," she said.

"I'm not certain about these black Wedgewood cups. Striking, but rather stark."

"*Anglais* design."

"However, they are truer to the original Greek than some of the French efforts I've seen."

"As no doubt are some of the practices of the house in which they are employed." Madame and I exchanged smiles. Considering how we almost shot each other in a duel whilst trapped in the Patent Office during last summer's invasion, we'd become rather decent friends. Mind you, my spare cash in exchange for her spare room helped that along. I could have managed the visit on my own, but I was glad that she was curious enough to accompany me. One lady seen entering Mrs. Woodley's establishment on a Monday morning might be mistaken for an enquiry of employment; two would more likely be construed as an inspection from a new female benevolent society for moral uplift. Or some such nonsense.

"Madame Serurier, I am honored. But, if you will allow me, surprised."

Mrs. Woodley's buttercup-and-silver dressing gown in the Chinese fashion coordinated well enough with the drapery, which is to say nothing in which either Madame or I would have been seen dead. But apart from that, I wasn't quite prepared for her to present as one's sweet little Southern auntie, the bit of gray and the few shallow wrinkles obviously providing the right touch of familial comfort to the clientele. My previous encounters with her profession had been at His Majesty's naval bases, and the clientele there definitely didn't buy from their aunties.

"And Mrs. Crofton, a pleasure," she said. "I seem to recall hearing something about those strange things you tinker with, if that's indeed what you still do."

Washington City's population may not be much in excess of twelve thousand, but unless my reputation had grown without my knowledge, someone had been telling Mrs. Woodley more about me than I cared to have told. Unfortunately, I had a perfectly good idea as to who that person was.

"Tinker would not, I fear, be an acceptable definition in Mr. Johnson's *Dictionary* for the term 'invent,'" I said.

"Forgive me, Mrs. Crofton. When you run a profitable business like mine, you tend to concentrate on literature that your patrons find entertaining," Mrs. Woodley said.

"Voltaire, for example?" Madame said. " And for the more romantic officeholder, a volume of Rousseau?"

I was guessing Marquis de Sade, but appreciating Madame's sense of diplomacy, I decided not to elevate the argument.

"I do my best to provide the most stimulating evenings I can for the District's free-thinking gentlemen," Mrs. Woodley said. "As you may have heard."

Much of what we had heard involved costumes and stage properties, and that book of scenarios available for a modest extra charge to those gentlemen less free of thought than others. What I imagined Walter Clarkson wrote in exchange for the occasional privilege of the house. Which gave me some pretext for pursuing a visit whilst Mr. Lightner and Mr. Dunn explored the Alexandria waterfront. Granted, I wasn't sure what I was looking for, but the house provided a common denominator between Clarkson and Mr. Dunn, and Clarkson was connected to the missing cheese, and Mr. Dunn had worked the Alexandria docks, where the cheese had last been seen.

All right, I suppose it was the vaguest of excuses to see where Mr. Lightner had spent some of his recreational hours, and I was afraid still did. But it was also the place where someone involved in a conspiracy to kidnap a cheese might say something about it in the course of an evening's scenario.

"It is one thing to hear about an establishment, and quite another to see it," Madame said.

"True," Mrs. Woodley said. "Though I don't tend to find calling cards from the city's feminine elite on my hallway trays. In fact, I believe you're the first ladies of a non-professional nature to actually pay me a call. So I might assume your visit to be in the nature of a philanthropic inquiry. And didn't I just read an announcement in the *Intelligencer* about the Washington City Orphan Asylum Society soliciting new members? Could they be in need of my funds after all?

Or have you come to rescue an orphan or two to get things off to a righteous start?"

"So long as we are getting straight to the point, Mrs. Woodley, the answers would be yes," I said. Madame raised her eyebrows at me. Mrs. Woodley nodded and smirked.

"As an astute businesswoman attuned to the sensibilities of Washington politics," I continued, "surely you can understand why Mrs. Van Ness, as a banker's wife, and Mrs. Brown, as a pastor's wife, didn't feel they could call on an establishment such as yours. And as for Mrs. Madison, well, she couldn't risk a national scandal at a time of postwar reconciliation, could she?"

"I imagine Dolly would just as soon have me shut down if it wouldn't trigger an impeachment bill against that stick of a husband," Mrs. Woodley said.

"Or from what I have heard, perhaps a second burning of the president's house," Madame said. She poured Mrs. Woodley a cup of coffee.

"But Madame Serurier and I are in a different position," I said.

"Now that's the logic of the grand dames for you," Mrs. Woodley said. "You're both foreigners, so somehow you have less to lose by seeing me. And you're willing to accept that to be members of their club. Seems like a high price."

Madame was not pleased, but she retained an even tone of voice in reply. "Mrs. Woodley, you know as well as I that the ladies of Washington City are always of a mind to follow the French."

"In dressmaking and dinner menus, maybe, but not in matters of morality."

"Ah, yes, there I suppose you may be correct. Those houses considered of highest quality here would not even serve on the waterfront in Toulon."

Mrs. Woodley glowered at Madame, setting down her cup with a fair measure of force. As a tribute to the Wedgewood factory, no laurels cracked off and the saucer remained intact.

"Of course, the men of the French naval service do have a reputation for being selective about the recreational facilities in which they pass time," Madame added. "I am sure that many Washington houses would profit handsomely in one of the rougher ports such as Naples."

Mrs. Woodley stood up. "Ladies, you must have more pressing frivolities on which to spend your day."

I stood in response, but Madame continued to sip coffee.

"Mrs. Woodley," I said, "I know how much you'd like to help the orphan asylum. Surely we can find some basis on which you could."

"This house wouldn't be appreciated in Naples," Mrs. Woodley said.

"My general impressions of that city did suggest that its inhabitants are characterized by a not inconsiderable degree of boisterous demeanor," I said, sitting us both back down.

"The Neapolitan fellow who was here Saturday certainly had that. Very rowdy."

"A Neapolitan? Really? I'm not aware of any men of that birth in the resident diplomatic corps. Are you, Madame Serurier?"

"I believe there is a Venetian on one of the staffs. He is partial to masks, so it is difficult to verify."

"He wasn't a diplomat," Mrs. Woodley said. "He wasn't much of a gentleman. In fact, it turns out that he wasn't ... " She poured herself a bit of coffee.

I knew Mrs. Woodley was in a quandary, since it would be highly damaging to admit that she'd mistakenly entertained a black man, even to us.

"Wasn't what?" I asked.

"This is absolutely confidential." Mrs. Woodley said. We nodded, and the three of us leaned forward. "He wasn't of the Italian race at all. He was black."

Madame and I both gasped, though I thought mine the more genuine. "Why Mrs. Woodley," I said, "he must have also been the proverbial master of disguise."

"Even better than the Venetian," Madame said.

"Well, you know how it is with some of them," Mrs. Woodley said.

"How what is?" I asked.

"Some of them have almost had the blackness bred clear out of them." Mrs. Woodley's grimace indicated the peculiar pain for Southern women of the "peculiar institution," a position I find impossibly hypocritical. In view of rumors about her own background, I believed Madame shared my sympathies.

"*Mon Dieu,* however then do you tell the difference?" Madame asked.

"Instinct. You know, that's all. Ultimately, you just know," Mrs. Woodley said.

"But you did not."

"It was Saturday. Business was very brisk. A large number of gentlemen wanted to continue celebrating the opening of the Washington Canal."

"How very appropriate. Celebrate a birth with a little death." I smiled, but Mrs. Woodley looked puzzled. And I'd have thought her an expert in sexual metaphors.

"Of course, under such conditions you couldn't possibly do anything other than rely on your instincts as a hostess," I said.

"I can't turn away good clientele. I do have competition."

"So who did rectify the impropriety?"

"The city marshal figured the man out."

"Then your instincts as a Southern lady hadn't deserted you after all, if you felt compelled to call for him."

"He was already here. And I have to tell you, he was having a very unusual night."

"Do you mean to say that he is not one of your more free-thinking patrons?" Madame asked.

"Let's say he's content with the basics, and doesn't generally add extras to the bill. But on Saturday, well, you should have seen the outfit he came charging downstairs in. We all had to bite down something fierce to keep from cackling at him."

"Court jester or Bo Peep?" I asked.

"You almost got it with the latter. He was dressed as a milkmaid. Wearing a papier-mâché cheese around his neck."

The three of us laughed, although I wasn't nearly as amused to find out that his partner in that scenario had been Mr. Lightner's very own friend, Anne Frederick.

Washington City marshal and young prostitute from rural Pennsylvania. They seemed an unlikely combination for high-level political extortion. But then, in the hierarchy of great powers, the United States is definitely low-hanging fruit. One has to start somewhere.

7

"You sure you don't want to look for a trail of crumbs? The worst that'll happen is we'll run into some old lady who'll try and cook us. I expect we could take care of that, even if you were only a member of the militia."

I would have told Charlie to behave himself, but I didn't want to do anything that he might interpret as an attempt to act as his master. As it was, I had to tell Mrs. Jenner that my new roommate was my new servant, and it took a lot of apologizing to get Charlie to swallow it. Washington City doesn't have a surfeit of lodging both habitable and cheap, and we both knew it wasn't worth risking his being rousted off the street on a vagrancy charge. But he wouldn't stand for being cooped up all day, so I now had a second partner in my increasingly less discreet search for the great cheese. This wasn't at all bad in case I encountered real trouble; the problem was getting Charlie in the habit of referring to me in public as "boss."

"Okay, then how about we just start at Gadsby's Tavern," he said. "It's getting cold standing out here and an ale or two would likely help that."

"Gadsby's is the last place in Alexandria to start asking questions."

"Anything you ask the cargo handlers will get up King Street to the cargo owners sooner than later. Might as well save time and be comfortable about it."

I shook my head. "I told you we have to keep as much of a lid on things as possible. Seems to me the discretion of an underpaid dock-worker is more persuadable than that of a prosperous merchant."

Charlie spat into the river. "You do have a lot of faith in human nature. 'Course, on your budget, you don't have much choice. So which of those fine gentlemen over there you want to start persuading?"

The Alexandria waterfront was quiet for a Monday afternoon: two small groups of men were unloading a fishing smack and a schooner.

"The smack?" I asked.

"The guys working the smack are likely the crew unloading their own catch, so they ain't likely to know much about unloading the cheese. And there's less bird shit to dodge on the schooner."

The men working the schooner weren't proficient in the art of conversation, but Charlie and I were an excuse for a smoking break. They'd heard about the cheese, and one of them had actually worked the *Geneva,* the ship that brought it from New York City. He hadn't handled the cheese, but I persuaded his brain to recall a man fitting Brackenridge's description yelling at his crewmates as they loaded a huge crate onto a wagon. Had the dockworker overheard where the crate was headed? No. Did the yelling man ride with the wagon? No. Dr. Thornton would probably disallow half the amount of persuasion when I submitted the day's expenses, but at least the dockworker had verified the basics.

Or had he? Brackenridge told me that while he and the *Geneva's* master argued over paperwork, the wagon had taken off and was too far down the road to chase once the argument was settled. Okay, maybe that's the sort of misunderstanding you get with a cut-rate teamster, and Brackenridge is certainly no long-distance runner. But why trust a stranger to deliver a precious cargo that you'd babysat all the way from Vermont? Brackenridge explained that he wanted to pay some calls while in Alexandria, and since the last leg of the route was the least hazardous, he'd seen no problem. No problem except that he couldn't recall the teamster's name—Dick something?—or much about him. And they'd not gotten around to signing any papers on the delivery. And as to the delivery? To save warehousing charges until January, Brackenridge had arranged to store the cheese with a friend in Washington City from his consular days. But his friend knew nothing more, and Brackenridge refused to give me the name.

So I was debating how much more persuasion was worth risking on the taciturn dockworker when another crewman spotted a bulky, slouch-hatted man limping his way towards the pier. The crew scrambled back to work and strongly suggested we get out of their way.

"Captain Peterman. Dock boss. You work here, you work through him," Charlie said.

"You could have mentioned him in the first place."

"Can't say as how the old bastard's a favorite of mine."

It wasn't hard to see why, as civility wasn't Peterman's strong suit any more than good grooming. However, free ale is free ale, and he deigned to join us in front of the fire in a workingman's tavern a block from Gadsby's. I would have preferred to talk in a less conspicuous area, but the direct warmth eased the discomfort in his leg, and I sensed that arguing with him wasn't the best tactic.

"Damn surgeon didn't set it right, y'see. A common midwife would've done better. Even Charlie boy could've."

I prepared myself to restrain Charlie from banging his tankard against Peterman's leg, but Charlie just stared into the fire and swigged his ale.

"I understand completely," I said. "I never can seem to shake a whole range of maladies. Muscle aches, head pains, digestive irregularities—I no sooner get one set under control than another crops up. But you visit a doctor, and all they want to do is bleed and purge, and what good does that do except make you feel weaker?"

"And poorer. Get yourself a good book of physic and treat yourself, I say."

"I have to agree with that."

"Well, you got a bit of sense, anyway. If the damn surgeon had, I'd still be master of a ship, not wrangling lowlife to move other masters' cargo." Peterman looked at Charlie, but Charlie kept still. I'd owe him a few more rounds before the week was out. "So who you chasing down? Escaped prisoner or runaway slave?"

"Neither one. As I said, I work for the State Department."

"If you was a marshal who didn't want a man to know he was trailing him, that might be one thing you'd say."

"Captain, I might wish to be doing something that adventurous, but the plain truth is that I'm on a simple assignment to verify some numbers."

Peterman held up his tankard for a refill, pinching the barmaid roughly as she poured it. I gave her an extra few cents for her trouble. "They made you trudge all the way down from Washington City for that?"

"Well, we weren't exactly sure who to write."

"What I make on my hires ain't the business of the State Department."

"I have no instructions about that. What I'm looking at has to do with ... mileage."

Charlie coughed, and shook his head.

"What's the matter, Charlie boy? Ale too strong?"

Charlie set down his tankard and stood, staring into the fire. "No. I'd say it was on the watery side."

"Turn around when I talk to you. Did you hear me, Charlie boy?"

"Captain, if we could get back to my numbers?" I said it in my most officious voice, but he and Charlie continued their standoff.

"What you been doing since I kicked you off the docks? Something that left cotton stuck in your ears?"

Charlie turned slowly to Peterman and put his foot on the arm of the bench where Peterman rested his leg. A few of the other drinkers looked over at us. I cleared my throat as loudly as I could. Peterman unhooked his leg from the bench. "Maybe you better go clean 'em out," he said.

"With your permission, Mr. Lightner," Charlie said with his eyes still fixed on Peterman, "perhaps I can find our guest something more suitable to drink. Something more gentlemanly, like a bottle of bourbon."

"Don't drink bourbon."

"No? Gentleman like yourself? Now, that surprises me, Captain. If I could afford good bourbon, I'd have it all the time."

"Which is why I wouldn't touch it."

Charlie raised his voice ever so slightly. "Captain, you mean to tell me that you can't stomach one of the finest products of the great state of Kentucky? A state whose sons manned the ramparts outside New Orleans, standing shoulder to shoulder with Old Hickory to drive the British from our soil, relying on that fine Kentucky bourbon to help them shoot straight and true? I mean to say, Kentucky bourbon wins us the war and all you'd do if presented with a glass of that most honorable liquid is turn up your nose?"

Peterman eased himself up. He was shorter than Charlie, but every bit as muscled. "Charlie boy, I don't give a shit about Kentucky or anything coming out of it. Now just what are you going to do about that?"

Charlie backed away from Peterman as the butt of a Kentucky rifle swung down in front of him and landed on Peterman's head. He turned to the rifle's buckskin-clad owner as Peterman collapsed onto the bench.

"Sir, I'm purely sorry you had to trouble yourself with that."

"No trouble," buckskin said, wiping Peterman's blood off his rifle butt.

"I believe my boss here would like to buy you a drink."

The tavern keeper just happened to have a good bottle of bourbon on hand. The price of that and a tip to the barmaid for tidying up the bench allowed us to leave before Peterman regained consciousness. We took bottle and buckskin to the riverbank. About half the bottle, two plaintive ballads and a sea shanty later, we discovered that buckskin was a teamster engaged in hauling freight from the back country. He thought he knew the cut-rate teamster who'd picked up the cheese.

At least I had a shot at justifying the day on my expense report.

8

Watching a man section a piece of fruit can provide a most interesting insight into his character.

Mr. Dunn takes the direct approach: a quick thrust with his knife, two unhesitant longitudinal cuts, and four pieces of apple are ready for consumption. Mr. Lightner studies a pear as if it were a block of marble, looking for exactly the right place in which to begin his peel. The pear is stroked with the fingertips, turned round, upended, turned right again, set back down for further contemplation. Granted, I've found similar sequences quite pleasurable when practiced on one's person, but on dessert, simply too fussy. I could make allowances for the eccentricity, but Mr. Dunn could not.

"Damn it, Mr. Horn Player! You gonna eat that thing or marry it?" He quickly apologized to Madame and me for the outburst. We nodded in sympathy. Our supper at the French Ministry was the first time the four of us had met since we saved the Patent Office, and the reunion would have been lovely but for Mr. Lightner's sullenness.

"I think Mr. Lightner still needs to express himself artistically from time to time," Madame said, though, as Mr. Dunn had risen to stretch his limbs, her attention was clearly not focused on Mr. Lightner's temperament.

"Well, then, find a horn and give us a tune, or recite some Shakespeare. But if you don't mind, I've been on short rations too many times to tolerate a man messing with his food."

Mr. Lightner held up his pear and took a large bite. "Better?" he asked. He and Mr. Dunn stared off for a good ten seconds before Mr. Dunn walked to the fireplace and lit his pipe. The pear wasn't the issue.

"Refresh my memory," I said. "This teamster you're looking for—what did you say his name was?"

"Coleman. Tom Coleman," Mr. Lightner said.

"Right. You have a description."

"From a man who was pretty sure he drank with him a few times somewhere in western Virginia. Maybe near Winchester. In your basic roadside ordinary that could easily be confused with a dozen other such places along your average set of cow paths."

Mr. Dunn tapped his pipe on the bricks. "Tall fellow, six foot and, oh, two or three inches, well over two hundred pounds, red hair down to his collar, full beard. Nose busted up, couple of missing teeth. Figure him somewhere around twenty-five."

"Which probably describes half the freight handlers working between the Appalachians and the Atlantic," Mr. Lightner said.

"I don't think half of them have red hair."

"Lots of Scotsmen breeding in the back country."

"Yet it is some basis on which to proceed," Madame said. She walked over to poke the fire, kneeling into a position that allowed the firelight to best reflect the sheen of her dark hair and show her firm breasts to their full advantage. I suspect that if heavy stays return to dominate fashion, she will be sorely disappointed.

"Madame, we're talking about days of travel between here and Winchester," Mr. Lightner said. "That's a great deal of territory for Charlie and me to slog through on the general recollections of a bourbon-soaked mule driver."

"I don't get it," Mr. Dunn said. "When we finished with our buckskin friend, you sounded like a man whose shovel just hit Blackbeard's treasure chest. About the time we crossed back over the Potomac, you sounded like you'd opened that chest and found a bunch of rocks. What's the matter? You still annoyed that I got Peterman whacked on the head?"

"He might have been a source of information."

"We got information. I don't think he would have told us anything better."

"We won't have a chance to find out, will we?"

"He was breathing when we left him."

"Fine. We're not sitting in the Alexandria jail on a murder charge. Or maybe the concussion did him in a few hours ago and there's a marshal out looking for us."

"Well if there is, he's my problem. You had nothing to do with it."

Mr. Lightner slammed back his chair and strode to the fireplace. Madame eased herself into one of the flanking wing chairs.

"Charlie, whether you like it or not, I'm now responsible for you," Mr. Lightner said. "You get into trouble, I get into trouble."

"You bailed me out of that cell, okay, I owe you for that. Got me some papers so I don't land back in, okay, I owe you for that. You let me sleep on your floor, okay, I've slept on worse and I owe you for that. I got to call you 'boss' to keep people from asking questions—okay, I find a way to do it. But I am not your boy, and you damn well better not forget it."

The four of us kept silent. Mr. Dunn might not contradict the occasional assumption that he was Italian and we might joke about it, but the fact remained that he wasn't white and Mr. Lightner was, and their natural instinct to jostle for supremacy was constrained by that fact. Except that Mr. Dunn's brief experience of command had taught him that power could be allocated otherwise, and Mr. Lightner had no experience of command at all.

"You can stop calling me 'Mr. Horn Player.'"

"Would 'Mr. Cassius' be acceptable?"

"Cass will do."

The corners of Mr. Dunn's mouth turned up a bit as he sat in the wing chair opposite Madame. "Nothing wrong with playing the horn, though."

I took Mr. Lightner's hand and led him back to the table. "There must be some way to narrow a search for the possibly corporeal Mr. Coleman," I said.

"I suppose we could retrace our steps and accuse the people we questioned on the way back of lying," Mr. Lightner said, fiddling again with his pear. "As a gunnery expert, what do you think, Charlie? How much buckshot could we tolerate before needing medical attention?"

"Depends on how fast you were running from the door when the trigger was pulled."

"Of course, they might be less inclined to shoot a woman."

"Especially if she was armed with a rocket."

I was not in the mood. "Whilst it might be amusing to test your hypothesis, Mr. Dunn, I'm afraid I'll have to decline. I have an equally important line of enquiry to pursue."

Mr. Lightner laid down his knife, leaving the poor pear in a crudely chiseled state of semi-nudity. "You might have said something earlier."

"I didn't think it worth disturbing the companionable quiet of the dinner table."

"Would you care to enlighten me now?"

"Actually, I wouldn't."

Mr. Lightner walked to the window opposite the fireplace, put his palms on the windowsill, looked outside, turned. Childhood training dies hard.

"Why is it that I seem to be the only one here taking the recovery of Brackenridge's cheese seriously?"

Madame, Mr. Dunn and I exchanged glances. "Mr. Lightner," Madame said, "it is, after all, only a cheese. An American cheese. If we were discussing, perhaps, a particularly rare Roquefort, there might be more cause for concern. But in that case, there would be more logic behind the theft, and you might not feel so lacking in direction."

"Madame Serurier, you of all people should comprehend the political implications."

"What I comprehend is that the United States is a young country which lacks, shall we say, a certain perspective. It has little historical context in which to place events, so everything may become a matter of national destiny. More to the point, although Washington City has the potential for some charm, it is not, you must agree, always the most stimulating of urban centers. Absent the war, and with the presidential election a year away, I suspect the cabinet is bored."

"So you're saying they've blown the thing way out of proportion?"

"I am sure they believe wholeheartedly in the gravity of the matter. Why, otherwise, would each of them have been so quick to evade responsibility for it?"

"Except for Dr. Thornton."

"Ah, well, William has motivations which run counter to theirs."

Mr. Lightner looked at Madame in that quizzical way intended to elicit further information without asking outright. It was a trick that came in handy when the subject was one's superior, but Madame knew it well, and declined to elaborate. She still guarded her friendship with the doctor as if it promised the emotional exclusivity she craved, even though I think she understood that it wouldn't.

"Cassius, no one's telling you to shrug the matter off," I said. "If the government thinks it has a crisis, then it has one until otherwise convinced. But that's no reason for you to become choleric or melancholy because you haven't yet found the contrary proof. Would you agree, Mr. Dunn?"

"It would make you easier to travel with, Cass."

Before Mr. Lightner could reply, Madame was summoned into the hallway by the insistent knock and rapid, high-pitched French pleas of her butler. "Well, Mr. Lightner, perhaps my analysis of *l'affaire fromage* was premature," she said upon re-entering. "One of my footmen has tripped and injured himself near the garden privy."

"Surely not on a crate of cheese," I said.

"On a man. Who, according to my butler, appears to be quite deceased."

"I must say that I'm relieved to see my knots intact. I don't get all that much practice these days."

Mr. Lightner was probably grimacing at me for that remark, but the lantern Mr. Dunn held was too feeble to illuminate much more than Walter Clarkson's leg. I have my way of dealing with death, and since Mr. Lightner hadn't volunteered to examine the body, I reserved the right to comment as I chose.

"Nice work at that," Mr. Dunn said. "You'd have made a good surgeon's mate."

"Or surgeon, if society and I had shared such an inclination."

"Do you see anything else of consequence?" Mr. Lightner asked curtly.

"Cassius, if you're feeling a touch squeamish, why don't you go back inside? I'm sure Madame's butler can find you something suitable to calm your stomach."

"I'm not feeling squeamish, thank you. I just think we ought to gather what facts we can and move the poor man to decent circumstances as quickly as possible."

"If I recall correctly from our last encounter with him, the two of you couldn't wait to be rid of each other."

"That doesn't mean we should leave him stretched out over the threshold of Madame's privy any longer than necessary."

I think Mr. Lightner was squeamish but couldn't bring himself to admit it. Good thing it was almost a new moon, though Clarkson's injuries weren't all that gruesome, and surely Mr. Lightner had seen worse during his brief time in battle. As he didn't care to talk much about it, I really didn't know.

"I wasn't planning to leave him here," I said. "I just haven't decided on the best way to conceal his murder."

"Are you totally ..."

I hushed Mr. Lightner before he could finish his comment about my mental clarity at a volume that would have attracted someone from down the street. We'd been lucky so far, partly due to the haphazard nature of Washington City development and partly due to the discretion of Madame's household staff. I didn't want to push that luck until we had some better idea of why Clarkson had gone from vertical to horizontal.

"I'm not suggesting that we heave him into the Potomac," I said, "or that we plant him beneath Madame's rosebushes." I looked up at Madame. "Unless you think he'd do the bushes some good."

"They are highly sensitive plants. I do not think they would take well to an aspiring journalist."

"I am suggesting that the constabulary can wait to muck things up until we've investigated further."

"I agree, Mrs. Crofton, but do you not think the matter would be best handled by French agents? After all, a murder on French diplomatic territory implies a threat against French diplomatic personnel."

"I fully appreciate your concerns, Madame, but as Mr. Clarkson had taken it upon himself to investigate the disappearance of the great cheese, it's more likely that he was following Mr. Lightner and me. Thus, it's best to keep this amongst us."

"You sure he was killed?" Mr. Lightner said. "He was balancing himself on a crutch and carrying a lantern. Wouldn't have been hard to stumble on a loose rock."

"Cassius, he fell away from the privy door, on which there is no blood, face down onto the grass. The back of his head is bashed in with sufficient depth to suggest a falling object the size and weight of, perhaps, a coconut, but you might observe that Madame has not seen fit to plant her back garden with coconut palms. We could be looking at a meteorite, but since no such showers were predicted in this month's almanac, I consider that possibility a miniscule one. Murder by blunt instrument is a thoroughly reasonable conclusion."

"And I think the blood on the crutch kind of sews that up," Mr. Dunn said.

"Which suggests a crime of opportunity," I said.

"Our privy is not intended for public access during non-business hours," Madame said, "but its location is hardly a state secret. Perhaps the gentleman was simply a victim of a random encounter."

"Robbery?" Mr. Lightner asked.

"Don't think so," Mr. Dunn said, feeling the pockets of Clarkson's waistcoat. "Still got a watch and some coins."

"How about a notebook and pencil?"

"Yeah. The notebook's blank. First few pages are torn out, though."

"Then they were taken. He was followed and killed by someone connected to the cheese-napping."

"Or he pushed his way into the privy ahead of someone with a weak bladder and a bad temper," Madame said.

"I doubt it, Madame."

"Cassius," I said, "considering that Mr. Clarkson thought he was investigating the most important story of his intended career, I suspect he was being secretive. It's possible that once he wrote something down, he left the pages at home prior to his next excursion."

"Got his key," Mr. Dunn said.

"Okay," Mr. Lightner said, sighing. "Now all we have to do is find the door."

"You don't know where he lived?" I asked.

"Walter had a minor philosophical problem with the concept of rent, so he moved around. And I didn't keep track. And if we start asking about it, someone will get curious. Isn't that what you want to avoid?"

"I know someone you can ask who'll keep quiet," Mr. Dunn said.

Who happened to run the last place I wanted Mr. Lightner to visit.

"Go on," I said. "Mr. Dunn can help us shift Mr. Clarkson to temporary quarters. The cellar, I should think."

"So long as he is well away from the wine," Madame said, leaning over the body to catch as much light as she could. "And before Louis returns, if you do not mind."

"I do not mind in the least," Mr. Dunn said, holding the lantern higher.

Solitaire for the English lady who doesn't ask certain questions.

9

Anne was indisposed.

Normally, this wouldn't have been cause for concern, as all of Mrs. Woodley's girls are inactive a few days per month. Cost of doing business, and a discounted bottle of champagne goes a long way towards soothing a customer put out by unavailability of a favorite. But something about this particular indisposition had Mrs. Woodley worried.

"It's not actually her … well, at least not according to Hannah," Mrs. Woodley said as we sat in the small room off her parlor that served as her office. Hannah did the girls' laundry, so her assessment was probably accurate.

"Digestive ailment? Some kind of flux?" I asked.

"I don't think so. She's not vomiting or complaining of any pain, and Hannah hasn't noticed anything amiss with the contents of her pot."

Thus no doctor had been called. The girls are most valuable, but bills are bills, a night call is extra, and a customer versed in bodily ailments who'll listen over a glass of claret is a cheap consult.

"Any fever?"

"She doesn't look flushed and she's cool to the touch. Truth is, Mr. Lightner, if she weren't one of my best girls, I'd think she was feigning the illness. And while we do sometimes have call for that sort of thing, I don't think she's working out a fresh scenario for the book."

Anne had been with Mrs. Woodley close to two years, not all that common in her line of work. She couldn't have been much more than seventeen when I first met her—the kind of pretty, petite, quiet country girl you hope to find on a farmstead or in a crossroads tavern at the end of a day's travel but never do. At least, I never seemed to while traveling in the company of my mother and sister. Which is why she became my favorite, and as my carnal preferences don't border on the peculiar, I became one of hers. Or so I was led to believe. Friendship under these arrangements is tenuous at best.

"What's she been eating?" I asked.

"That's just it: she hasn't been. I didn't think much of it on Sunday, but after another whole day, it doesn't seem right."

I had the distinct feeling that Mrs. Woodley wanted me to take a look at Anne, but with Walter's corpse on my mind, I didn't want to. Superstition, maybe, although I'm not normally superstitious. But somehow, if I examined Anne and she fell sicker, I'd feel responsible. Well, all right, I'd never seen her out of sorts, and if I did, it would spoil things.

"So I think it's providential that you came by this evening," Mrs. Woodley said in her best honeysuckle voice. "You being one of her very favorite gentlemen and all, I'm certain she'd appreciate a few moments in your company."

And you'd appreciate any further medical opinion I might render free of charge.

"As I said earlier, I really need to get along to Walter Clarkson's."

"Surely Mr. Clarkson can wait a bit."

Depending on his rate of decomposition.

"Besides, even though I do pride myself on knowing the particulars of my clientele, we are such a popular establishment that there are times when a piece of important information about any one gentleman just clear slips my mind. Like an address."

"This is the best time of year in the country. Apple harvest."

Lying in bed with a patchwork quilt pulled up to her neck, no rouge on her cheeks, no trace of perfume, talking softly about the Pennsylvania farm on which she grew up, Anne could've been my little sister taken with a slight cold. Or anyone else's. And like a little sister, the most she allowed me was a reading of her pulse. The pulse was normal; the demureness was unsettling, as were the flatness of her voice and the blankness of her stare. Mrs. Woodley's instincts were correct – this wasn't role-playing.

"Do you like apples, Cass?"

They're not my favorite fruit, but I sensed that wasn't the right thing to say. "Doesn't everyone? It's un-American not to."

Anne didn't smile at that as I'd hoped, but continued to stare in the direction of the window opposite her bed, not speaking for quite a few moments. The faint sounds of laughter and creaking bed ropes from the neighboring rooms suddenly seemed incongruous, and I began to feel uncomfortable.

"Which kind do you like best?" she finally said.

Not being my favorite fruit, apple varieties weren't high on the list of my educational priorities. But I had to say something better than "red." "Oh, I don't know. That's like asking me whether I prefer blondes or brunettes."

No response. The Anne I last saw a couple of weeks back would have teased me into confessing that her shade of auburn was the most appealing, and wouldn't have been afraid to employ various articles of underclothing in the process. Whatever this Anne was wearing beneath the quilt, I wasn't going to see.

"How about your favorite?" I asked. "What should I look for next time I'm in Pennsylvania?"

"Spitzenburg."

That was all she said for maybe five minutes. Town or apple, I wasn't sure, and I was reluctant to prompt her for clarification. If her behavior amounted to some form of female hysteria, it was beyond my competence. I was about to go downstairs and tell Mrs. Woodley to ante up for a proper physician when Anne spoke.

"President Jefferson's favorite. Mr. Jefferson loved the Spitzenberg, and my father loved Mr. Jefferson, so he went all the way to New York and brought back seedlings. I was a little girl then. We had our first good crop four years ago. Nice, big fruit with bright red skins splashed with streaks of orange. They're an eating apple. Oh, you can bake them into pies, too—my mother and I added them to the Pippins and the Baldwins. And they make fine apple butter. Crisp, yellow flesh, the sweet smell of the juice telling you it was time for harvest and all the good things that happen with it."

She stopped again. Okay, maybe this was some sort of confession. Apples and Eve, of course, so maybe she felt it was time to tell me about her fall from respectable womanhood. With Thomas Jefferson as the Devil? Anne wasn't the political metaphor type. And whatever the story was, why now? Tearful or otherwise, the reason a woman turns professional isn't usually laid out for a customer. Unless it's part of a game.

But she wasn't playing a game. And I was still a customer, albeit much less frequent. Had she decided to leave Mrs. Woodley's and was this some strange farewell? But then why take to her bed? Did she think she was dying?

"You can't eat or bake or preserve all the apples, of course. A well-tended orchard will give you barrels of them, and my father was very careful with his trees. So you make cider. Do you like cider, Cass?"

"Some of the toughest choices of my life have been between good cider and good ale."

Still no smile, but she kept talking.

"A good cider is harder to make than a good ale, I think. Getting the blend of juices just so, balancing the Smiths and the Russets against the base of the Baldwin juice, that's tricky. Adding the Spitzenberg—my father didn't want to try that the first year. We had a better crop the second year, though. A whole new flavor to blend. Like I said, it was tricky."

She paused again. "And dangerous," she added before closing her eyes.

10

Walter Clarkson's notes didn't mention shoes.

Not directly, anyway. I drew the inference from his mention of footsteps, and thus his suspicion that he was being followed. After we'd moved his body and Madame and Mr. Dunn had retired for a private conversation, I'd inspected the bare patches in the grass behind the privy and found two faint sets of footprints. One would have been Clarkson's. The other was smaller and narrower, but not clearly male or female, and like his, suggested nothing more than the usual plain leather sole common to footwear of either sex. I would have preserved them in plaster of Paris, but didn't want to rouse the entire Serurier household by rummaging for the ingredients. An early morning rain shower that obliterated them was the reward for my courtesy, which left me with only Clarkson's notes for clarification.

Unfortunately, they were graphically and grammatically untidy writings, most of which involved crude newspaperish code. For example, his note about keeping an eye on "t" followed by two stars followed by the letter "k." "Turk" was obvious, as in Samuel Brackenridge's stint as a consul to the Ottoman Empire. Clearly, Clarkson thought he was being clever by not simply using "S star star B star star idge." I never like to speak ill of the departed, but I can't say that the editorial world suffered a grievous loss when Clarkson's crutch found its way into the back of his head.

Nor, apparently, had Washington City. In the few days following his murder he hadn't been sorely missed, which was just as well for us, as we hadn't been able to shift the body from the cellar of the French Ministry. Good thing Madame, Mr. Dunn, and I knew the details of the Battle of Trafalgar. Not that we agreed on the propriety of the outcome, mind you, but on the ingenuity of the cleanup. We concluded that if temporary interment in a barrel of rum was not an embarrassment for Lord Nelson, it would suffice for Clarkson. Or in Clarkson's case a barrel of whiskey, as that was the preferred spirit on offer at the ministry for American visitors and a drink not avidly pursued by the Seruriers. As the Kentucky and Tennessee delegations weren't on the dinner schedule for two weeks, it was a reasonably safe course of action.

Madame, however, did have other things diplomatic requiring her attention, and Mr. Lightner had paperwork requiring his. Dr. Thornton had signed off on the expenses for Mr. Lightner's jaunt to Alexandria on the understanding that further day-long absences would be kept to an absolute minimum. If I hadn't known Dr. Thornton to be unyielding in his devotion to keeping the Patent Office running at all costs, I'd have been a bit suspicious of his truncating Mr. Lightner's investigative time. But I'd have needed far more than that before I suggested that he had anything to do with the disappearance of the great cheese, let alone Walter Clarkson's demise.

No, my line of enquiry still focused on a possible connection between the city marshal and Anne Frederick. Having not met either, I couldn't rightly estimate their relevant foot sizes to compare with my memory of the smaller footprints. I did have one clue, though: I didn't recall the smaller prints having an outline that, like Clarkson's, would have indicated enough wear to mold into left and right shapes. So those shoes were new, or nearly so. Clearly, some hands-on examination was needed, and what better place for that than S. Dunham Walker's recently opened shoe store on Pennsylvania Avenue? Somewhere in his "general assortment of shoes (principally Philadelphia make)" there was a potential match. And perhaps a nice Morocco half-boot.

"Madam will notice particularly the suppleness of the leather. Like velvet, wouldn't you say?" Mr. Walker, imprudently lacking shop assistants, was darting in and out of the curtained area behind his counter with armfuls of shoeboxes, splitting his attention between myself and several pairs of ladies, one or two with maidservants in tow. Box, comment, next lady.

"They look flimsy to me," Mr. Dunn said. I'd brought him along in the absence of a maidservant, figuring that he needed the morning out and that I might need a witness. I have had male proprietors of shoe shops become more than allowably interested in the architecture of my instep. If you're alone, he denies it; if accompanied by a female friend, well, given the choice between boycott or new shoes, she'll favor her foot. I'd borrowed a footman's coat from Madame to explain Mr. Dunn's role, but he wasn't entirely comfortable in it. The glances from the other ladies didn't help, though I thought them of envy rather than scorn.

"The box is put together good," he said, lifting it up and running his hand along its bottom. "Sanded smooth, no gaps in the joinery. Could be a Philly shipwright doing some night work. Shape it and put a sail on it, might make a worthy model for a river race."

"If I make a purchase, you may have the box. Mr. Lightner could borrow a model cannon for it from his office."

"I wouldn't ask. He'd be liable to requisition the box for his filing."

True enough. Thomas Jefferson himself had initiated the peculiarly practical system of storing patent papers in shoeboxes, but they weren't a prominent item in congressional appropriations bills, and they weren't easy to procure with dignity.

I rolled the top of the boot between my thumb and forefinger. It was good-quality kid, buttery to the touch and tanned to a lovely chocolaty brown, but Mr. Dunn had a point: not the best footwear for everyday use. Unfortunately, the funds upon which I draw were not in a state of growth, so something sturdier was a better choice. And that got me thinking.

"At least we can eliminate a boot like this one," I said.

"Why? The sole's thin, but they ain't moccasins. They'd still make some noise."

"On a floorboard, yes, assuming a sufficient amount of clumsiness or heaviness on the part of the wearer. But grass and dirt would likely muffle the sound. Now, if the leather were thick and stiff, you might hear creaking as the wearer flexed his or her feet."

The birdlike Mr. Walker flitted by on his way to the curtain. "Shall I write those up for Madam?" he asked.

"Perhaps something a bit more substantial for comparison," I said, and he sighed and flew away with his boxes.

"You wouldn't expect him to wear anything thick and stiff, would you?" Mr. Dunn said.

"Brocade slippers aside, he does seem to be more the dancing pump than brogan type."

"And not likely to confuse the two." Mr. Dunn and I smiled at each other, remembering poor Mr. Lightner's day on the battlefield in tight dancing pumps. He'd reached for them in the dark instead of his boots during a sudden and confused call to arms, and suffered the consequences. But as I'd made my first inroads with him whilst treating his blisters, the consequences weren't all bad.

"So we can probably eliminate Mr. Walker as a suspect in Clarkson's death," I said.

"Great. Lots of progress there. Only eleven thousand nine hundred and some suspects to weed out, not including the visitors."

"My point is about type. We still don't have any clear indication of which gender we're dealing with. Sorting by weight of shoe tells us that a man of Mr. Walker's sensibilities isn't likely to be who we're looking for." Very well, it wasn't exactly Newtonian physics, as the expression on Mr. Dunn's face pointed out. But what else did we have?

"Madam should find these quite acceptable. Red Moroccan, fastened by laces combining the delicacy of a dressmaker's ribbon with the strength of rigging rope. Absolutely the height of desirability amongst the ladies of Society Hill. Or dare I say, Mayfair?"

"You may dare, Mr. Walker, but that doesn't guarantee my belief."

Another sigh. "Madam may wish to examine the pattern circling the top of each boot, tooled in the Arabian fashion. Might that not make Madam feel like Scheherazade herself?"

"You are the daring man, Mr. Walker," Mr. Dunn said before I could reply. "You sell a shoe like that to a woman and it don't work out, she might demand your head on a dish."

Mr. Walker, shocked by the impudence, could only snort, gather his boxes, toss his hair, and sweep back to the curtain as I admonished Mr. Dunn loudly for everyone's benefit. Cloying proprietor or not, a new shoe store is not an establishment to which one wishes to be denied access, especially in Washington City. The other patrons frowned at me; the maidservants smiled at Mr. Dunn.

"Charles?" Mr. Dunn whispered to me.

"It goes with the coat," I whispered back. "And you did confuse Scheherazade with Salome."

"Sorry, Mistress. That mean I gotta leave the big house and go back to the fields?"

I felt myself blush. Before I could apologize, Mr. Dunn grinned and picked up one of the red Moroccans by a shoelace. "Strength of rigging rope, huh?"

"Careful, please. I'm not sure I can afford them."

"Good heft to them, though. Sturdy. Might just creak a bit while being broken in."

"So perhaps the person following Clarkson was a woman wearing something like these."

"She'd have to be strong enough to have given that crutch a healthy swing. Cass said that Anne had bottled herself up in bed well before the murder."

"And if she's feigning her indisposition after all?"

"As an ex-actor, I expect he'd be able to spot that kind of thing."

"Not necessarily when dealing with a woman with whom he's been, shall we say, overly friendly."

Mr. Dunn didn't reply right away. I think he was wary that I had an ulterior motive in wanting to implicate Anne Frederick, and he didn't care to reinforce it. He may have been right.

"So assuming the city marshal has bigger feet than this, maybe we're looking at a woman familiar with the process of cheese-making," he said.

"It does take some muscle to push a big paddle through a vat of curdling milk. But if I might not afford these, surely a dairymaid couldn't."

"Unless you're the kind of dairymaid who's real nice to a fellow with a bit of cash."

Of course, in terms of sound, any new pair of strong leather shoes would have done, which still left us the possibility of a small-footed man with more traditional preferences than S. Dunham Walker. Yet Mr. Dunn's logic was compelling. Who but a dairymaid would best know how to care for a valuable cheese while her patron? lover? negotiated its ransom? Except that in my experience, women didn't lean towards head bashing as a means of dispatching someone, at least not in peacetime. Obviously Mr. Dunn's experience of women was somewhat different.

"Take this hypothetical dairymaid, then," I said. "Wouldn't a woman used to the country be averse to prowling around a city at night?"

"Maybe not if she knew the city."

"So we'd be looking for a woman who worked on a farm within a radius of Washington City sufficiently small to allow her frequent visits."

"With a pair of sturdy new shoes."

"That could well have blood stains on them, but would be too valuable to destroy."

Pleased with ourselves, we both pondered that.

"Got to admit," Mr. Dunn said, "I never have known a woman who'd really kill for a pair of shoes."

Yes, Mr. Dunn's experience of women was different from mine. But not Mr. Walker's. Surrounded as he was, he knew that the only thing he could afford to do as I left without making a purchase was to sigh yet again and invite me back.

11

If I hadn't known better, I'd have said I was being disciplined. I understand there are military punishments where prisoners are forced to stack and re-stack cannonballs until they drop from exhaustion. Granted, shoeboxes are generally lighter than cannonballs, but the principle seems the same. For reasons known only to him, Dr. Thornton instructed me to immediately reorganize our filing system and after three days of effort, he was still dissatisfied with the aesthetics. Well, I'm not sure there's much you can do when inconsistent procurement policies leave you with an odd assortment of containers, and the number of boot-size papers accumulates in inverse proportion to the number of slipper-size boxes.

I don't think he ever got over the rejection of his design for the Capitol. I think his real reaction to its burning was a feeling of vindication. But Dr. Thornton hasn't survived as a staunch Federalist in two Republican administrations by overexposing such sentiments, so this wasn't about showcasing his architectural sensibilities for the visiting public. So why was I being kept at my post? Surely our cheesenapper was growing impatient, and sooner or later, Frenchy Nordin would notice that Walter Clarkson's bar tab wasn't getting any bigger.

At least Amanda and Charlie were out nosing around, although I couldn't say I was sold on their theory of investigation. Even if they found their mysterious Cinderella, what could we actually prove? As Samuel

Brackenridge said, not every farm woman's good at making cheese, ergo a particularly adept dairymaid might well earn enough money to indulge in new shoes. On the other hand, anyone willing to kill for the price of a pair of shoes would be willing to lie about it, and as for any unwashable bloodstains? Go prove they weren't from the late family pig. But maybe there was something to it. Better than what I was doing.

Ergo? If I didn't take a break, I'd soon find myself at the District courthouse begging permission for a license to practice law. I got up from the floor, stretched, and looked out the window at a flock of geese flying through the morning drizzle. Maybe Dr. Thornton would like the shoeboxes arranged in a "V" formation. We could tout it as a daring inversion of the classical pediment. Garner him more design commissions. Keep him away from the office.

I squatted a few times to loosen my knees. Then I realized I was being watched.

"Mr. Lightner?"

The soft male voice was hesitant. It sounded vaguely familiar, but I couldn't immediately connect it to a person. The same proved true of the face. Young, pale and indistinct. Like the clothes: plain gray coat, plain buff trousers, plain white cravat, plain, well-worn black shoes.

"I'm John Randolph."

Didn't ring a bell.

"John C. Randolph, actually."

Still no chime.

"From Treasury. I believe we have met."

He didn't look like a tax collector, nor did his demeanor exude the confidence of a man authorized to grab money from your pocket. And I didn't owe any customs or excise duties. Still … No. It couldn't be. Not the bottles of French brandy. That was years back, and anyway, it was Father's treat, not mine. I helped him pack, though. Stuff them into Falstaff's jerkin, I said, who'd notice the extra padding? Yeah, but they can't prove it was my idea, let alone my hands on the burlap. Can they? Has there been some advance in chemical solvents I've glossed over? Where'd they find the sacks? Where else? Mother's too frugal to have thrown them out. How do you like that? One short trip to Canada and your whole career is shot. Why didn't we win the war up there and annex it like we were supposed to? Damn New York militia.

"You paid a call on our department some months ago," Mr. John C. Randolph said.

Did I?

"Following up on a requisition for a new inkwell," he continued. "Glass, uncut, size category two. With an extra cork stopper. If approved, to be paid out of Treasury account S 1."

That visit. Randolph's face emerged into the hazy light of vague memory. Not long after the burning, after Congress graciously expropriated our offices and moved us into even tinier quarters, some petty German noblewoman knocked the inkwell off my desk while bending to examine a prototype mechanical washtub. In the interest of good foreign relations, it was determined that she wasn't liable for the breakage, and it took some debate to determine whether I'd be allowed to petition for a replacement at government expense. There was all that rebuilding to do, after all.

"I notice that you do have an inkwell," Randolph said.

"Stoneware, undecorated, size category barely adequate. With only one stopper. Paid for by the account of Cassius Lightner."

Randolph peered at the piles of papers and shoeboxes rapidly overtaking the floor. "I hope the inkwell size differential is not impeding the work of your office. If it is, you could send us an appending correspondence detailing the problem. Special circumstances sometime hasten the approval process."

He was definitely a career man. I apologized for the disarray and offered him the lone visitor's chair, which he took primly.

"Now that Congress is ready to convene in its new temporary building and you've been moved back into your original quarters," he said, "it's clear that your current temporary inkwell is disproportionate."

"May I take that as good news?"

"Quite possibly." There was a trace of excitement in his voice, which indicated that the trace of sarcasm in mine had gone the way of a dim firework. He glanced around and leaned in for a confidence. "In fact, bearing in mind that, although I am in charge of the distribution of stationery and related implements, as an assistant clerk I'm not authorized to certify final disposition on procurement requests, I could say with some confidence that the changed circumstances in the housing of your agency subsequent to the filing of your original petition for inkwell replacement could weigh very favorably."

Did I sound like that when answering an inventor? I hoped not.

"So your visit is a follow-up to my follow-up," I said.

"Collaterally, yes."

I waited for him to say something more. The excitement of almost committing himself to a possibility might have worn him out, but it was hard to tell.

"So there is another matter?" I asked.

"Oh, um, yes, yes there is." Randolph rooted around in the leather portfolio on his lap and removed a sheaf of papers bound in red ribbon. Quarterly returns. My favorite.

"These returns for the third quarter of last year. I'm afraid there are a few things that need reconciling," he said.

An inter-departmental audit. Great. I was tempted to grab my coat and hurry out the door, muttering something about saving the Republic, but I valued my job, and I wasn't sure that saving the Republic would balance dodging an audit. Besides, there was the new inkwell to consider.

"Whatever I can do to help," I said.

"I appreciate that." Randolph glanced again at the mess of shoeboxes and papers. "I can see that I've caught you at perhaps not the best time …"

"I am in the middle of a vital reorganization. Top priority."

"Indeed. I'm afraid I'm in a similar position. I'd have delayed the audit due to certain things on my current agenda, but my supervisor insisted."

"I understand."

"Thank you. Now, first off, I believe we may have a problem with the address listed for the Patent Office."

Oh, dear. Maybe I had a tooth that needed an emergency pull. No, I had to be the odd child who liked salt over sweet and remembered to brush. And who'd spent spare time hanging around apothecary shops trying out tooth powders.

"The postal building—formerly Blodgett's Hotel—E Street Northwest, between Seventh Street and Eighth Street," Randolph said, quoting last year's form.

"Is that not correct?"

"In substance, partly yes and partly no."

"That is an accurate description of the building in which we're sitting. The postal clerks never have any problem sending our mail to the correct cubbyhole."

"Well, yes, I can see that they might not, but then they do occupy premises in this building. One could reasonably assume familiarity on their part with a neighboring agency's location."

One could, couldn't one. One could also reasonably envision the effect of the application of one of the larger shoeboxes to John C. Randolph's skull. However, one murder by blunt object in my life per week was enough.

"Then what's the problem?" I asked.

"Well, um, lack of specificity."

"What?"

"According to my notes, your office relocated its quarters during the last half of the third month of the quarter. You failed to indicate that change."

"We only moved to another floor. And we never indicated the floor in our address in the first place."

"That in itself is insufficient justification for not indicating the change. You also failed to fill in the reason for the move. That should have gone on this line here."

I picked up a quill and dipped it none-too-carefully in my undersized inkwell, hoping to splash a drop or two onto Randolph's plain gray coat. The ink missed the coat. Without stopping to blot my desk, I quickly scratched in the words, "British burn city. Congress kicks us upstairs." Randolph turned paler.

"Now Mr. Lightner, you should know you can't amend a report that's already been submitted simply by writing on it. That's strictly against Treasury regulations."

"I don't care! You wanted a reason, you got it!"

Randolph took a handkerchief from his coat sleeve and wiped the emerging sweat from his forehead. I wouldn't have guessed lace trim to be to his taste. Maybe it just had a lot of holes from overuse.

"Mr. Lightner, I didn't come here to provoke an argument. I am charged with verifying the accuracy of all agency reports pertaining to the quarterly consumption of paper, ink, quills, and paraphernalia peripheral thereto, and I do intend to carry out that charge to the utmost of my abilities."

I remembered why I didn't remember him. Randolph reflected the dark impulses lurking in all government clerks, and as with any ugly reflection, the mind recoiled. But this wasn't the time to fight reflections.

"Call me Cassius."

"In the middle of an audit? I don't think that that would be right."

"Please. In the spirit of inter-departmental cooperation. After all, we are brothers. Of a sort."

Randolph thought on that for a moment.

"Thank you. I ... I'm much obliged." He hesitated again. "I suppose you could call me John."

I was afraid I had acquired a new friend. Hopefully, he wouldn't ask me to meet him behind some woodshed to exchange drops of blood.

"You know," he said, "you're the only person in the service who has extended me the courtesy of first names. Even the other assistants in my department haven't done that, and we've worked together for many years."

"Some departments are more formal than others."

"No, no I don't think that's entirely the case. But we should get back to these third-quarter returns."

"By all means. First, I think a glass of Madeira would be in order."

"On duty?"

"Patent Office custom. We find that moderate lubrication of the brain matter facilitates comprehension of technical specifications."

Randolph's shock gave way to wide-eyed curiosity as I ducked into Dr. Thornton's office and returned with two filled glasses. He took his gingerly.

"To inter-departmental fellowship," I said, toasting him.

"Yes, yes, absolutely to that." He glanced towards the door before allowing himself the daring on-duty sip.

"Your fellow clerks must think very highly of you," I said. "Your attention to detail is staggeringly professional."

"Thank you. I do try to be accurate. Not that everyone doesn't strive for accuracy."

"Not everyone achieves it at your level. I haven't."

"Oh, well, a chief clerk like you has so many things to keep an eye on. It's quite understandable why you might omit a change of floor. Your assistant should have spotted the omission before he sent over the returns."

"He should have. Unfortunately, the position's been vacant for some time."

"Really?" Randolph's eyes widened again as he dared a second sip of Madeira.

"But there aren't any present plans to fill it. And anyway, Treasury's got to expand faster."

"Do you think so? People seem to be inventing so many things these days."

"Exactly. The more inventions, the more commerce, the more commerce, the more settlement, the more settlement, the more territory the federal government has to administer. Federal departments will expand their consumption of paper and ink at an exponential rate, not to mention peripheral paraphernalia. Treasury will have to answer that growth with more personnel, and that has to mean promotions. And for someone with your level of accuracy ..."

The poor man looked like he was about to cry. "You honestly think I might have it in me to make chief clerk?"

"Written in the stars." Of course, as my namesake said, the fault lies not in our stars but in ourselves, and Randolph had "permanent assistant" written on him in triplicate. However, there wasn't any point in being rude, not with an audit to avoid.

"It's very good of you to notice," he said. "No one else seems to. Well, that's not entirely true. Mr. Brackenridge has expressed similar sentiments."

Firebell.

"I'm not entirely familiar with the chain of command at Treasury," I said. "Is this Mr. Brackenridge a sub-departmental supervisor?"

"No. You must know of him, though. He's the gentleman who's brought the great cheese down from Vermont."

Maybe this wasn't going to be such an unproductive morning.

"Ah, yes, that Mr. Brackenridge. A very enterprising gentleman, indeed. One of those men determined to drive the engine of commerce forward into that upward spiral of plenty I was talking about. I'm not surprised that he's spotted your potential when your less dynamic colleagues haven't. Have you known him long?"

"In a way. I handled some of his paperwork when I first joined the department. He was a consul, you know. In the Ottoman Empire, no less. And one of my first tasks was to proofread his supply requisitions. Imagine. Proofreading the correspondence of a United States consul. And writing back!"

Imagine. And to think I'd handled the man's patent application.

"Oh, I must say, I hold a great admiration for those in the diplomatic corps," Randolph said. "The work must be so challenging."

"I'm sure Mr. Brackenridge has told you some exciting stories."

"Our – that is to say, his – correspondence was very businesslike. Facts and figures."

"Then you've never actually met?"

Randolph swallowed the last of his Madeira and put down his glass. "No, no, I've not had that honor."

"Now I'd think that you'd be one of the first people he'd have sought out on this visit to Washington City."

He wiped some more beads of sweat from his forehead.

"I'm sure he's very busy, what with preparing the great cheese for its unveiling," he said.

"That's not for months. And how much work can it take to drape some bunting around a cheese?"

Randolph gave out a little forced laugh.

"It is twelve hundred and fifty pounds. That's a great deal of crepe," he said.

"I'm sure he'll have help."

"A man as important as Mr. Brackenridge? Yes, of course."

"In fact, I'll bet he'll be in touch with you yet."

"I ... I'm not very good with decorations."

"Nonsense. You've handled his correspondence. I'm sure he'd have complete faith in your ability to handle his cheese. Once he divulges its whereabouts."

"What do you mean?"

"Just that the cheese has been out of the news for awhile. Almost as if it had disappeared."

Randolph quickly gathered up the offending quarterly return. "Mr. Lightner, I very much appreciate your hospitality, and I'm terribly sorry, but if you don't mind, I'm afraid we'll have to finish our review of these papers at another time. There's another matter ..."

"Whatever best suits your schedule."

"Thank you. Thank you, I'll be in touch." Randolph backed out the door, fastening his portfolio as he went.

Nice leatherwork. Fancy tooling around the edges. A little expensive for an assistant clerk.

12

Why is it that when a man can't sleep, he insists on you sharing the insomnia?

He should have been able to sleep. Minister Serurier's diplomatic business had left Madame in Mr. Dunn's company for an evening of cards, Mr. Lightner and I had shared a pleasant roast duck supper prepared by Madame's chef in exchange for my not playing cards but testifying that I had if necessary, and a light rain provided soothing background noise. And our lovemaking had been at least as pleasant as the roast duck.

Of course, the duck was just a bit dry.

At any rate, I was able to drift off quite easily. If there were a correlation between the decoration on John C. Randolph's portfolio and the decoration on the red Moroccan boots I chose not to purchase, I was content to figure it out after breakfast. But not Mr. Lightner.

"It's too much of a coincidence," he said. Half awake, I murmured a noise or two in assent, hoping he'd turn over and let me sleep.

"The boots and the portfolio have to be from the same place."

"Mmm-hmm."

"Now, the owner of the shoe shop – what's his name?"

I muttered something to the effect of "Walker."

"Amanda, are you listening?" As he was shaking my arm, I'd reached a point of consciousness where I had little choice but to pay attention. I rolled onto my back, trying to avoid eye contact, or any further suggestion of desire.

"S. Dunham Walker," I said.

"Right. Walker said the boots were decorated in Arabic …"

"Fashion. In an Arabian fashion. No actual letters."

"Yeah, yeah, okay. An Arabian design. But you can't remember the actual pattern?"

"It was something geometric. I'll try and draw it for you in the morning."

"I'll light a candle." As he tossed off the quilt and sat up, I grabbed his shoulders and leaned my head against the back of his neck.

"Cassius, my sweet, the cabinet is asleep. Congress is asleep. In the hills near Charlottesville, the president is asleep. It's a reasonable supposition that our cheese-napper is asleep. I should very much like to join them."

"Oh. Sorry. I didn't realize I was keeping you awake. You go back to sleep. We'll get it in the morning." I thanked him, kissed him, and drew us down under the quilt. Mr. Lightner's breath against my ear combined with the raindrops into a lovely soporific. For a few lovely moments.

I sat up.

"You want to draw it now?" he asked.

"No, I'm trying to work out a design for a mattress and suspension system which will allow two people to share a bed without the movements of one affecting the other. We'll make a fortune."

Mr. Lightner took the candle on his nightstand over to the fireplace and poked around for an ember.

"Did we leave any of the Bordeaux?" I asked.

"Only some residue."

"I'll take it."

Mr. Lightner brought me the wineglass and began to pace.

"Are you about to ask Hamlet to avenge you, or are you about to frighten the Scottish usurper?" I said.

"What?"

"Your walk with the candle. The professional poise is unmistakable."

"Sorry. You know how it is when you get an idea in your head at this time of night."

"My love, when was the last time you saw me doing an imitation of Anne Boleyn's ghost?"

"I'm not the one who relies on sleeping potions."

"Only because you're afraid they'll upset the rhythms of your digestive system."

"Maybe I should walk you back to the ministry so you can get some rest."

"No, come and sit. Let's see if we can't reason your brain into a cooler condition." I finished the dregs of the Bordeaux, propped myself against the headboard and wrapped the quilt around me as he did so.

"Randolph's an assistant clerk, and from what I gather, not too high up the ladder," he said. "Even allowing for better salaries at Treasury, he must make less than I do."

"Well, at least someone does. That's comforting." Mr. Lightner's frown invited an apologetic kiss. I wasn't in an apologetic mood.

"My point being that a man making, say, seventy-five dollars a month isn't going to be buying expensive leather portfolios," he said.

"He may have family money. Remember, your background is more the exception in the federal service than the rule."

"Thanks for reminding me."

"Don't mention it."

"Okay, if he has family money, why dress so plainly?"

"Perhaps he's a Quaker."

"Virginian, I think. Not too likely."

"Then perhaps he's simply a man of solid republican principles, who doesn't want to appear aristocratic. Didn't Mr. Jefferson sometimes choose a plain coat and old slippers when receiving European dignitaries?"

"Mr. Jefferson has his quirks."

"I wouldn't say that too loudly. You never know who might be listening."

"Walter's still dead, isn't he?"

"Whiskey's a preservative, not a restorative."

"Mr. Jefferson aside, if Randolph had money, he'd show it. An expensive ring or watch-chain at least. Something to distinguish him."

"Very well, then. Let's assume that Randolph didn't buy himself the portfolio. Award for meritorious service?"

"Even less likely than his being a Quaker. No, I think we can reasonably conclude that it was a gift."

"From S. Dunham Walker?"

"From Samuel Brackenridge."

I had to ponder that one, which required a bit of pacing.

"The quilt works well enough for a royal robe, but I think you need to tuck your head more under your arm," Mr. Lightner said.

"Don't be cheeky." I'd spent the day spying on farm women without stepping across anything more incriminating than cow dung, and I wasn't in the mood for his smugness at getting ahead of me.

"Just trying to bring your efforts up to professional standards," Mr. Lightner said. "You'll get along better with the family that way."

I might have teased a proposal out of that remark, but I just didn't feel like doing so. "How do you figure that the pattern in the leather suggests Brackenridge?" I asked instead.

"His time in the Ottoman Empire. It's not only the kashkaval cheese he likes. He admires their art as well."

"He only said so in passing. That doesn't necessarily make him a devotee."

"You don't have to collect paintings or sculpture to be interested in a piece of fancy leatherwork."

I came back over to the bed, took paper and pencil out of the nightstand drawer, and sketched what I remembered of the design on the Moroccan boots: four little leaves surrounded by a thin line, repeating in a band around the edge. "Something like this?"

"That's it."

"I'm relieved to know that my girlhood art lessons weren't taken in vain. Still, all we've established is that two leatherworkers share the same taste in oriental decoration."

"Or one. It could be the boots and the portfolio were made in the same shop."

"So?"

"So if we trace the boots, we might be able to trace the portfolio, and then see if Samuel Brackenridge bought it."

"The boots might be from Philadelphia – Walker advertises that most of his stock is. But even if it turned out that Brackenridge bought the portfolio there, we can't wait at least a week to confirm that."

"No."

"And what would it really prove, anyway?"

Both of us pondered that, without pacing.

"It's leverage, isn't it?" Mr. Lightner said.

"On whom? Brackenridge is the victim here. What, you think John C. Randolph stole the cheese?"

"I don't know. He certainly didn't lift it himself. But he's connected with Brackenridge in some way that he doesn't want to admit. And I'm not so sure that he wasn't trying to get more from me than changes to a form."

"Such as?"

"Seeing where I was in my investigation."

"And how would he know you were looking except through Brackenridge? Anyway, he just doesn't sound like the type to involve himself in this kind of blackmail."

"What if he and Brackenridge have a relationship they'd prefer to keep hidden?"

"As in the passing of bribes?"

"Possibly. I was thinking of something more personal."

"Such as?" I knew to what practices he referred, but I wasn't sure it was a good idea to let him know the extent of my understanding. There are still matters about which even an enlightened man like Mr. Lightner prefers his lady to feign some ignorance.

"Things that sailors do. Occasionally. On a long voyage," he said.

"Scrimshaw? I should think they'd be proud of that. Unless they're not very adept."

"Something more personal."

"What could be more personal than artistic expression?"

Mr. Lightner answered with a look indicating that he didn't want me to make him spell it out.

"Oh," I said as demurely as I could. I believe the Lightner family might find my mimetic abilities reasonably satisfactory.

Mr. Lightner nodded. "And then if that somehow ties in with Walter's murder ..." I put my finger to his lips.

"I think that's enough theorizing for now, don't you?" I said, unlacing my nightdress.

Eventually, he saw things my way.

13

There's good reason why Francis Scott Key's new poem is best sung after a few drinks.

I, for example, having a trained voice with a reasonable range, strain to reach the high notes of the middle passage without screeching. All right, I was trained by my mother, who wasn't exactly the product of the best European tutors. However, we did manage to please audiences only too eager to register their displeasure with shotguns and knives, something which choirmasters like Bach and Handel never had to face. So while Mr. Key's poem may well deserve continued public recitation, it doesn't deserve continued public humiliation because no one has thought to fit it to a better tune than that of an old English drinking ballad. Not that the tune's a bad one. As an instrumental in the hands of the Marine Corps Band, it works well. But these days, patriotic audiences can't be convinced to leave well enough alone.

Hopefully, they can be convinced that *Hail, Columbia* makes a more appropriate national anthem if Congress ever decides to adopt one. If Key hadn't gotten inspired, it would have remained the odds-on favorite. Then I suppose you could say that if Key hadn't gotten inspired, it would have been because the British took Fort McHenry, and I wouldn't have been spending my Saturday afternoon on the grounds of the president's house listening to the weekly Marine Band concert.

Amanda insisted. Oh, I love the band – they're one of the few public cultural pleasures on offer in Washington City, and I attend whenever I can. Sometimes I even imagine myself among them, though my brief experience with the District militia tells me I'm not cut out for the Marine Corps. But they do look sharp in their brilliant red coats, and, if truth be told, there are times when I miss performing. Not enough to return to the stage. Enough for the occasional small lump in the throat when one of the horn players takes a solo.

Having finished *Anacreon*—excuse me, *The Star-Spangled Banner*—the bandsmen arranged their music and did some re-tuning for the next selection, although how they could tell who was off-key in the jumble of voices and instruments eluded me. Like the rest of the crowd, Amanda took the opportunity to converse as she adjusted her camp stool to provide a more solid seat on the moist dirt.

"Now, unpolished introduction aside, isn't this a more effective use of the afternoon than trying to inebriate a Treasury clerk?" After some sleep and some breakfast, she wasn't convinced that I'd get anything worthwhile out of John C. Randolph that wouldn't prove embarrassing for all concerned. I wasn't convinced that spending the day prowling more farms in search of incriminating footwear would be any more productive. She compromised on the concert.

"If my theory about him is correct, it's probably better than giving him the wrong idea," I said. I'd stumbled into that scenario in my teens, and didn't want to repeat it. "But it's been a week. I do have to come up with something."

"And we shall. A couple hours of music will relax the brain and make it more receptive to a keen insight." So far, neither of us had made much sense out of a missing but not necessarily real teamster, a dead man's oblique reference to footsteps, and an exotic leather pattern suggesting a possibly unmentionable relationship. Maybe something in Mozart's *Gran Partita* would help.

Two familiar voices sounded behind us. They weren't going to help me think better.

"William, you must admit that it is an unusual selection for such a large number of musicians."

"Madeleine, the Marine Corps Band is very versatile. I'm sure if Herr Mozart had them at his disposal, he would have arranged the piece to take advantage of their depth."

Madame Serurier had arranged herself as elegantly as possible on the canvas seat of her stool and was studying the program broadsheet. Dr. Thornton fussed with the proper relationship between the position of his stool and the position of his walking stick. Neither spouse was present, which wasn't unusual for her but was less so for him. At least she hadn't brought Charlie.

"Mr. Lightner, what do you think? Surely the extra contingent of horns will overpower the clarinets," she said, her eyes still fixed on the program.

The four of us exchanged greetings.

"Mr. Lightner, don't you have other matters requiring your attention?" Dr. Thornton asked.

"William, allow him to answer my question, if you please," Madame said.

Dr. Thornton harrumphed and moved his stick an inch to the left, looking somewhat like a surveyor about to take a measurement of the field.

"They have additional clarinets as well," I said. The opening chords of the *Partita* then rumbled over us with all the resonance sixty-odd wind players can generate. In fairness to Madame, the brief clarinet solo sandwiched between the first and second set of chords did sound thin.

"You understand my concerns," Madame said after the third set of chords. The clarinets and oboes began their trade of solos over supporting bassoon. When the brass chimed in, they blended well.

"The horns do seem to be giving the reeds due deference," I said.

Amanda shushed me. Dr. Thornton looked like he was about to do the same to Madame, but gestured at me instead. The bouncy main theme was off and running, and not to be missed. Well, if you did, you'd catch it on its way back. Mozart's nothing if not symmetrical.

After many variations on a theme, the band reached the final three notes and received a round of enthusiastic applause. The drum major took his bow, the bandsmen took theirs, and all dispersed to the band tent for their break. Some of the men in the audience wandered to the edges of the grounds to relieve themselves. Some of the ladies looked uncomfortable but remained seated. They do seem to have the tougher time at public events. As always, Amanda had an eye on the problem.

"You know, Cassius, every time we attend a concert I become increasingly convinced of the profitability of a large-scale business in portable privies," she said.

Dr. Thornton answered her before I could. "Draft a design, Mrs. Crofton, and I will be only too happy to examine it. It might induce Mrs. Thornton to rekindle her interest in band music."

"I should think such an enterprise could be quite a risk," Madame said.

"I disagree," Dr. Thornton said. "At a penny per person, the concert season can't help but make money."

"I was thinking more of potential injuries." Amanda and I both looked at her in alarm, but she just smiled back.

"Now really, Madeleine, who injures himself while using a privy?" Dr. Thornton said.

"Mrs. Crofton, you have some knowledge of the healing arts. Would you say that the risk of injuring oneself in a privy is negligible?"

Amanda hesitated before answering. "Madame Serurier, perhaps this isn't the best subject to pursue during a concert interval," she said.

"On the contrary, I think a public event is often the best place to explore delicate matters." Madame smiled at Dr. Thornton. He fished his watch out of his pocket for a quick look. The band had a few minutes.

"Well, then," Amanda said, "I suppose the level of risk would depend on one's threshold of pain. I have known more than a few able seamen with only a child's intolerance for a splintered bottom."

"So, William, at least we may conclude that a privy can be a dangerous place for a sailor. And Mr. Lightner, you have a good deal of experience with roadside lodgings of the meaner sort."

"Unfortunately, I do."

"And would you say that the average traveler passing through these establishments has a substantial chance of relieving himself without a scratch?"

"Fifty-fifty at best."

"So now, William, it seems that we can add at least one further category of person for whom a privy could become a veritable chamber of horrors."

Dr. Thornton looked unamused. "The band members are heading back to their chairs," he said. "What's next on the program?"

Madame turned the broadsheet in her lap face down and folded her hands on top. Two trombonists cleaned their slide tubes, pipes of smoldering tobacco still in their mouths.

"In fact, I would imagine that people have even met their deaths in privies," Madame said, looking straight into Dr. Thornton's eyes. He didn't flinch.

"A case of sudden apoplexy is always a possibility," he said, a touch of anger in his voice and a touch of red in his face. He never liked being on the losing end of one of Madame's argument games. Question was, did the anger come from anything else?

"But for whom?" Madame said. "For an old person, surely. I would not think so much for a younger person. For example, a young man accustomed to nightly walks."

"Madeleine, precisely what is your point?"

Madame held Dr. Thornton's stare for another moment then turned away to study her broadsheet. The clarinetists had returned, and reeds were being re-tightened.

"The Gossec symphony should be interesting," she said.

"Madeleine, you started this argument. Finish it!"

"I must say, I hold a certain admiration for Monsieur Gossec. His ability to capture the sound of the revolution after working for years under noble patronage reminds me of the considerable skill of my husband in assimilating new philosophies of government."

Dr. Thornton stood up suddenly, knocking over his walking stick. The heavy silver knob hit the ground barely an inch from Madame's foot.

"William, you should be more careful. I imagine that is the sort of accident which might very well injure a young man on his way out of a privy."

The drum major flipped through his music. A bassoonist ran a scale amid the random notes popping around the trumpets. Dr. Thornton, redder and tight-lipped, retrieved his stick.

"Mr. Lightner, Mrs. Crofton, would you be kind enough to see Madame Serurier back to the French Ministry?"

"You do not care for the Gossec?" Madame asked.

"Not at the moment," Dr. Thornton said, and walked away. The drum major raised his baton.

"I think there is something he is not telling us," Madame said as she folded her broadsheet. Amanda squeezed my hand. The band commenced the *Military Symphony in F.*

Sound of the revolution, indeed.

14

"You sure that's the right tool?"

"If I were, my love, I'd be a lot wealthier woman."

Mr. Lightner grunted in response to my irritable tone of voice, and snuck another look through the window blinds.

"A woman who designs rockets should be able to defeat a simple lock on a desk drawer," he said.

"I'd be happy to design one and blow the thing apart if you'd prefer."

"Just hurry it up, okay?"

My immediate thought was to consider where else I might insert the bullet probe with which I was working, but I kept it to myself. It was late, we were both tired, my knees were sore, and Mr. Lightner had begun to flinch every time I shifted my weight and made the floorboards creak. Triggering a full-blown row was not going to help get us into Dr. Thornton's private files.

"I'm sure the good doctor is tucked into bed with no intention of returning until Monday morning," I said.

"We don't know that. It was odd for him to be working well into a Saturday night. Maybe he just went home for a quick snack."

"Would you rather leave?"

"We have to see what's in that drawer. If I'm being set up, I need to know it now."

"Then stop nagging at me and let me get on with it."

Unfortunately, the lock mechanism was proving to be more stubborn than expected. I'd chosen the probe over a more cumbersome jackknife and a more delicate hatpin, but it was only an approximation of a proper lock pick. Charlie Dunn was a better mechanic than I, but Mr. Lightner didn't want to have to explain him if caught. So I was left to do the best I could, handicapped by inadequate light and a fidgety accomplice. After several more minutes of fruitless tinkering, my level of frustration was outracing my sense of adventure.

"I suppose we could just get an axe and be done with it," I said.

"Or we could just go over to his house and yell 'murderer!' That would get his attention, too."

"Dr. Thornton did not kill Walter Clarkson."

"Why not?"

"Well, for one thing, I don't believe him capable of it."

"You don't work with him on a daily basis."

I stood up and stretched, hoping to relieve the stiffness in my knees. "Your imagination is getting the better of you."

"You saw how he reacted at the concert."

"Madeleine was having her fun, that's all."

"Very specific fun. She knows something she's not telling us."

"Anyone else you'd like to add to this conspiracy? General Jackson himself, perhaps?"

Without answering, Mr. Lightner took my place at the desk and began to jiggle the bullet probe. I took the opportunity to rest in Dr. Thornton's pleasantly rounded Windsor chair, and had just about nodded off when Mr. Lightner began to curse.

"Are you sure you don't want an axe?" I said.

"No, I do not!"

"Temper, my love. The night constable might be within earshot."

At that suggestion, Mr. Lightner braced himself against the desktop and kicked the offending lock with the heel of his shoe. As I might have warned him, the kick simply drove the probe deeper into the keyhole, from which position it did not care to be removed.

"Bastard!" he growled. "He must've designed the damn thing himself. See what I mean?"

"Not exactly."

"A reasonable man would have trusted a normal lock. Something a normal person could break open. A man who won't trust a normal lock is fully capable of committing murder."

"You really do need to lie down."

"Maybe I should get Charlie."

"He may not want to be disturbed."

Mr. Lightner banged his hand on the desk. "You know, one of these nights, he's going to find himself on the wrong end of one of Louis Serurier's pistols."

"I doubt it. Diplomats don't care much for scandals. And Madame is very careful with the official schedules. Besides, as far as we know, she simply finds his skill at cards more enjoyable than mine."

"So what else would you suggest?"

"I suppose we could break into a blacksmith's and borrow a pair of tongs."

"How long do you want us to spend in jail?"

"Us? You kicked it."

Mr. Lightner suddenly held up his hand to quiet me.

"What? What is it?" I whispered. He tiptoed across the room and held his ear to the door. Getting no further response, I did the same.

Footsteps. Faint, but discernable.

"Boots," I said.

"I don't care if they're ballet slippers. We're trapped!"

"Not necessarily."

"Are you crazy? There's no way we can drop out of that window without breaking more than a few bones."

"Well, we both won't fit under the desk."

More footsteps, followed by the rattling of one of the ground-floor doors.

"That's not Dr. Thornton," I said.

Mr. Lightner gingerly opened the door.

"Where are you going?" I said.

"To lock the front door. Something I should've done half an hour ago."

"No. Whoever it is will hear the turn of the lock."

"So?"

"So if it's the night constable, he'll find the sound suspicious."

"More suspicious than finding the door unlocked?"

"Maybe he's only checking the ground floor."

"True. He might be too drunk to make it up the stairs."

The boots began to climb the stairs.

"So much for that theory," I said.

Mr. Lightner hurried to the desk and took the candle. "Stay here," he said. "I'll sit at my desk and shuffle some papers. Problem solved."

"Unless it's not the night constable."

"Who else would it be?"

"Walter Clarkson's real murderer?"

The boots reached the top of the stairs. Mr. Lightner shoved the candle into my hand, ran to the fireplace, and grabbed the poker. I backed myself to the desk and grabbed the only other suitable weapon in the room. It had been years since I'd swung a decanter of Madeira at anyone. I hoped I wasn't too out of practice.

The doorknob to the front door turned. The door creaked open. A small beam of light spilled onto the floor.

"Hello?" A country drawl, lower-range baritone. "Main door downstairs was open. Figured you might still be workin'. Hello?"

The boots clomped towards us. Mr. Lightner brandished the poker. I hefted the decanter, trying not to spill the wine. The door to Dr. Thornton's office swung open.

The man carrying the lantern was tall and solidly built, with long red hair and beard, and a nose that looked a bit out of joint. When he greeted us again, I noticed the missing teeth.

"Mr. Coleman," I said, lowering the decanter. "What an unexpected pleasure."

15

So the buckskin from Kentucky hadn't spun a tall tale. There was a Tom Coleman. Word had gotten around in the last few days that some federal man was looking for him. That place where they keep the models of the newfangled things. Not the older fellow.

Trouble was, Tom Coleman didn't have a clue as to the whereabouts of the great cheese.

"I swear on my mama's fancy bible, I dropped that crate right here. Smack under the hayloft. Keep it more outa the rain and all. See? What else you think made this big rut in the ground?"

Sure enough, the rut did suggest the outline of a crate large enough to hold a twelve-hundred-and-fifty pound wheel of kashkaval. Amanda, Charlie and I were agreed on that. What we hadn't agreed on was the plausibility of Tom Coleman's story.

"Mr. Coleman," Amanda said. "Whilst I do not doubt that your mother maintains a copy of scripture in a condition decent enough to provide sufficient foundation for an oath, I'm not convinced that the rut wasn't simply laid out with a shovel."

"Pardon, ma'am, but I didn't drag you two miles outa town in the middle of the night just to show you that Cousin Ray don't much like to paint his barn."

Cousin Ray didn't much like to patch too many of the smaller holes in the roof and walls, either, but the padlock on the door was free of rust, and in good working order. Set back from the main road and obscured by the dilapidated farmhouse it once served, the barn wasn't exactly the sort of place where a casual traveler would expect to stumble across a giant crate of cheese. I could see why a cut-rate teamster would figure it to be a cost-effective storage facility. I could also see why Amanda and Charlie, trained to the standards of modern naval procurement, were more skeptical.

"Maybe we ought to go talk to Cousin Ray and make sure this is his barn," Charlie said.

"He's off huntin'," Coleman said. "No tellin' when he'll get back."

"'Course he would be."

"You callin' me a liar?"

Charlie stared Coleman down before answering. "No. Just admiring Cousin Ray's horse sense." He turned away from Coleman and began an inspection of the walls and roof.

"Now, Tom," I said, "you did mention that only you and your cousin had keys to this place."

"Yes, sir, I did that. Ain't nobody else has reason to."

"And only you and he unloaded the crate from your wagon."

"That's right."

"That is rather a large amount of dead weight to be shifted by just two men," Amanda said.

"I haul freight for a livin', ma'am. I do know how to set up rollers or a ramp."

"Still," Amanda continued, "allowing for the crating and packing material, that is, what? Nearly seven hundred pounds per man?"

"Ray can bend an iron bar bare-hand. Two if he ain't drank more than half a jug."

Coleman looked over at Charlie, who continued his slow pacing of the perimeter of the barn. "And I can take Ray in a fight."

"After how many jugs?" Charlie asked. Coleman moved towards Charlie.

"Mr. Coleman, my assistant's detached to me on his current service from a position of considerable rank with the navy. That would make two government departments authorized to negotiate with civilian contractors."

Coleman stopped. "Okay," he said. "I done my part bringin' you here, even if the crate's gone missing. So how about we talk some of that extra business?"

"As soon as we clear up a few more details."

"See, I didn't get but half my fee. Don't get the other half until I haul the crate into town. But how am I gonna get that other half if there ain't no crate to move?"

"How long were you supposed to keep the crate here?" Amanda asked.

"Don't know, exactly. I don't think more than a few days."

"And then where were you supposed to take it?"

"I ain't been told yet." Coleman spat some chaw.

"Did Mr. Brackenridge say anything about a friend of his when you picked up the cheese?" I asked.

"Not that I recall."

"So he simply told you to bring the cheese here and await further instructions," Amanda said.

"That's all. He made sure the crate was safe on my wagon, paid me my half-fee, and left."

We quickly turned towards the sound of boot heel cracking through wood.

"What the hell are you doin'?" Coleman shouted.

"Just a little test," Charlie said. He'd kicked through a section of barn wall hidden behind some hay bales. "Whoever built this barn didn't do too bad a job. The original wallboards are pretty solid. Much thicker than the wood patching up this big hole."

Coleman put his lantern up to the wall and carefully ran his fingers along the broken boards.

"What do you think, Mr. Coleman?" Charlie said. "Look like Cousin Ray's handiwork?"

"It don't. It ain't mine, neither."

Charlie handed me one of the broken boards. "Smell that."

I took a good whiff of the board.

"I'd bet that's fairly new cheese," I said, and handed the board to Amanda.

"With a hint of sheep," she said.

16

That mantle clock is getting on my nerves. There's something about the "tock" that's not quite right. Needs tuning, I should think. A few moments more, and I fear I shall rip out its pendulum and throttle it into silence.

All right, I'll try and restrain myself. I really don't want to be responsible for plunging the world back into war by destroying a bit of French government property in a fit of impatience.

But understand this, Miss Frederick: with Mr. Lightner missing and very likely in mortal danger, my patience is hardly infinite. I promised Madame Serurier that in her absence, I would not leave you in my bed unattended, and so I will not. So long as you continue to breathe, however fitfully. However, as you refuse to cooperate by taking even a bit of water, let alone communicate by other than the briefest unintelligible vocalization, who's to say exactly when that breathing ceased, except me?

That lovely, plump spare pillow would solve the problem, would it not? I could search for Mr. Lightner with a clear conscience. I don't think the coroner would ask too many questions, what with Madame testifying that your breathing had already slowed when she left you in my charge.

So what shall we do, Miss Frederick? Are you going to take some water and rejoin the world, or shall I assist you in leaving it?

17

"Damn, Cass! You don't keep your backside in one place, I'm going to give it a real good introduction to one of these oars."

"Sorry, sorry. Just trying to get a better view downstream, that's all."

"I just don't want a better view in-stream, okay?"

The Potomac can be a nice place on which to spend a sunny Sunday morning. Admiring the trees, sipping wine, holding hands—that sort of morning. This morning was about not snagging a tree branch in the fog while grabbing the occasional swig of whiskey to fend off the chill. Charlie kept his hands on the oars; I kept mine on a spyglass.

"Still don't get why a man like Brackenridge would head out in this stuff to catch a few fish," Charlie said. "From what you described, he don't sound like the sporting type."

"No particular reason for the desk clerk to lie."

"Could be Brackenridge gave him more than half a dollar."

"I don't recall you volunteering anything extra."

"I ain't officially on the payroll."

And at this point, I didn't know how much longer I'd be on it. Amanda had volunteered to try and extract the bullet probe from Dr. Thornton's desk so long as I didn't help. Coleman had volunteered to hunt down Cousin Ray, and made it clear that it was strictly family business. Charlie, ever the careful mariner, had volunteered to wait for Brackenridge in McKeowin's hotel bar. A sensible approach, to be sure, but I wanted to find Brackenridge before a tree branch found him.

If, indeed, he was on the river.

He'd lied to me when he told me that he'd had the cheese sent from Alexandria to an old friend in Washington City. So maybe Charlie was right: bribing the desk clerk to fend off inquiries wasn't beneath him. If he hadn't lied to me, then Tom Coleman had when he said that Brackenridge told him to take the cheese to the barn. But none of us thought Coleman was lying. In fact, despite Coleman's assurances to the contrary, we were afraid that Cousin Ray might be due for an unexpected hunting accident. All the more reason to talk to Brackenridge as soon as possible.

"You getting tired, Charlie?"

"I'd have to guess that's your tactful way of asking why we're slowing down."

"It had crossed my mind."

"Don't suppose you've noticed that we've turned against the current."

"I didn't realize we'd gone that far."

"We're about to row into the Eastern Branch. We've patrolled about as much riverbank as Brackenridge'd be likely to set up in, unless you think he's heading down to the bay to hook some deepwater fish."

"I doubt it."

"So unless you want to hook some deepwater fish, I figure we'd best head back upriver."

"The desk clerk said he told Brackenridge the fishing was better in this direction."

"And if he wanted to send us the wrong way, where might that put Brackenridge?"

"Somewhere near Mason's Island?"

"That'd be my guess."

"Fair enough. But let's check around the island before we check the taverns on the Georgetown waterfront."

"Whatever we bump into first, captain."

It was Mason's Island. Charlie may have a mind of his own, but he's honest enough. We found a rowboat beached against some trees on the side of the island that doesn't face Georgetown. Whoever had taken out this boat wanted privacy. But unlike ours, its paint suggested an easier life than that of a short-term hire. There wasn't any fishing equipment in it, either.

"Brackenridge ain't the kind of man partial to perfume, is he?" Charlie asked.

"He wasn't on the day I met him."

"Well, if it's his boat, he's not here for the fish."

Brackenridge and a companion? On a Sunday morning rendezvous? If the companion happened to be married, the island would make sense, and the fog would provide an extra measure of protection. Most women would insist on something more comfortable, though. So who'd value secrecy over comfort?

Randolph? Were my suspicions about him and Brackenridge right after all? I didn't recall Randolph wearing any particular scent, but then I'd only met him on official business.

"Scent's not too strong, so it's hard to tell, but there's something familiar about it," Charlie said.

Eau de gunboat? I didn't think things in the navy had gone that far.

Charlie took out his folding knife. "Maybe there's something of interest in this little provision box."

"Should you damage that padlock, I presume you are prepared to reimburse the French government," said a voice from the trees. A very familiar voice.

"Now Mrs. Madeleine, you know how careful I can be," Charlie said, grinning.

"Mrs. Madeleine?" I said as she walked over to the boat.

"'Miss' doesn't fit," Charlie said.

"And by now, 'Madame' seems too formal," she added. She perched herself on the stern of the boat, managing to adjust her cloak for both warmth and Charlie's benefit. Charlie sat in the bow seat, which enabled him to look slightly downward towards the stern. I remained on my feet, feeling a little like a footman at a royal picnic.

"I note Mrs. Crofton's absence," Madame said. "Is she well?"

"She's fine," I said.

"A day out for the boys. My apologies if I intrude. Although, as you are equipped neither to hunt nor fish, I am curious to know what I have intruded upon."

"Search party," Charlie said.

"Is that so?" Madame said. "Are there other boats on the way?"

"Just ours," I said.

"I see. A matter of discretion. *Mon dieu*, something embarrassing has happened to Minister Serurier. And on the day that my butler has off!"

"Sorry to disappoint you, Madame, but Charlie and I weren't out looking for you."

"No? Are you sure?"

"Quite."

"Oh. Well, you must forgive me, but when one is found by the premier tracker of cheese in Washington City, one must assume the object of his search is at least as valuable as a cheese."

I really didn't like being teased by Madeleine Serurier. I was never sure how seriously I was being taken.

"We're looking for Samuel Brackenridge," Charlie said.

"Out here?" Madame said. Her surprise was slightly overdone. Charlie didn't seem to notice, but then I was better schooled in the new theories of realistic acting than he was.

"Clerk at McKeowin's told us he went fishing," Charlie said. "The island's a good spot for it."

"Especially if you don't want to be disturbed," I said.

"Then if that is his intention, do you not think he is entitled to it? It is Sunday, after all." She'd turned defensive, and it was genuine.

Hold on. Madame and Samuel Brackenridge? No. Couldn't be. She already had Charlie for clandestine amusements and Dr. Thornton for public ones. Admittedly, I was not a sophisticated young Frenchwoman casually neglected by her husband, so maybe I didn't really understand, but Brackenridge? Corpulent, wheezy Brackenridge? All right, I got annoyed at Amanda when I thought she'd been overly friendly with the man, but that wasn't about sex, it was about business.

Business. Was that it? Something like Amanda's rental arrangement at the French Ministry that enriched Madame without the French government taking its cut?

What if he hadn't lied to me? What if Madame were the old friend from his consular days?

"Madame, you wouldn't happen to have seen Mr. Brackenridge in the area, would you?" I asked.

"And if I had, how should I have recognized him?"

"Cass tells me he's a good-sized fellow, around – what'd you say? – forty, forty-five," Charlie said, light and easy. No reason yet to prompt Madame into tightening her cloak.

"Around that," I said.

"Light or dark hair?" Madame asked.

"Dark brown. With some gray starting to show through."

"And does he bear any special features? A large mole, or perhaps a dueling scar?"

"Not in any place proper for me to notice."

"Then I have not seen him."

"Then whom have you seen?"

"Mr. Lightner, there is no call for you to be cross. I row myself out here for a pleasant solitary walk and what I receive is an interrogation. If anyone has the right to be irritated, it is I."

"If you were out for a walk, how come you were watching the boat?"

"Cass, you got your answer."

"Not entirely. I think your doubts were correct, Charlie. Why risk taking out a boat in bad weather for sport? You could sit in McKeowin's lobby and drop a line into one of the mud holes on Pennsylvania Avenue. And as for walks, there are plenty of nice trees near the French Ministry."

"Mr. Lightner, it is not for you to question how and where I choose to take my exercise." Madame glanced at Charlie and tightened her cloak. Charlie glowered at me.

"It isn't," I said. "Except it does seem more than coincidence that both you and Samuel Brackenridge decided to brave the fog and row to Mason's Island."

"We don't know that Brackenridge was headed here," Charlie said.

"We don't. Although it was your logic that suggested it. Excellent logic, too." I sat on the boat opposite Charlie. Both of them studied me for a few moments before Madame broke the silence.

"Mr. Lightner, I have no better idea of the whereabouts of the great cheese than you."

"Madame Serurier, in no way have I suggested that you're involved in its disappearance."

"You may not have suggested it, but perhaps you have been toying with the idea, no? You pursue Mr. Brackenridge to this island only to find me instead and you think, ah, she must be waiting for him. And why that? Does she have some information for him? Something for which he would pay good money?"

"Do you?"

Madame smiled. "If I do, telling you would not serve my purposes, so we must proceed on the basis that I do not. However, as you, Charles and I are allies, I will say that Mr. Brackenridge and I did arrange to meet here this morning. I will also mention that he is overdue for the appointment."

"We didn't see any wreckage," Charlie said. "But I wasn't the one with the spyglass."

"It may simply be that Mr. Brackenridge is not as efficient with an oar as you," she said. Charlie smiled and she stretched, loosening her cloak. Getting the hook out of his mouth wasn't going to be easy.

"Madame Serurier," I said, "appointments are either for business or pleasure. If yours doesn't involve business …"

"Let us say it involves friendly advice."

"Then you do know him."

"We have exchanged letters."

Charlie walked over to Madame and leaned his face next to her ear.

"Mrs. Madeleine, in all fairness to Cass, you should have mentioned that last week."

Well, now. The hook wasn't in as deep as I'd thought. Madame looked surprised. Maybe she'd forgotten that I was the one keeping Charlie off the auction block.

"Charles, if the matter were pertinent to his investigation, I would have done so."

"Why wouldn't it be?"

"Because I say it is not."

"I think you owe us a better answer than that."

She stood up and slapped Charlie in the face. "You presume far too much on our acquaintance, Mr. Dunn." She gestured for me to get out of the boat, then pushed off and rowed it away.

"Must be the onions I had with breakfast," Charlie said.

"You want to follow her or wait for Brackenridge?"

"Be a while before Brackenridge gets back to McKeowin's. I'd rather rifle his belongings and see if we can't find a few letters. You got some more money for the clerk?"

First Dr. Thornton, now the French Minister's wife. What the hell. My family and I had only performed *The Beggar's Opera* once, but I think I remembered enough to be credible in my new career.

18

"Brackenridge? Corpulent, wheezy Brackenridge? Surely not."

"She claims it's business," Mr. Dunn said. He sat in Mr. Lightner's wing chair, puffing on the last third of a slim Spanish cigar, the lone survivor of a gift packet from Madame Serurier. He looked none too happy. I hadn't realized that he'd actually formed some sort of attachment to her in the brief time since his release from jail. Perhaps he hadn't realized it either.

"I'd believe business," I said. "She's not averse to making her own money."

"Kinda got that feeling from the way she handles cards."

"Yes, she does hold with a rather flexible interpretation of the number fifty-two."

"Of course, she and I didn't play for cash."

"Well, I'm sure she didn't want to take advantage, what with you being kind enough to volunteer your services for us."

"Oh, I don't know. Most women don't wear three pairs of stockings this time of year."

Mr. Dunn removed the cigar from his mouth, frowned at it, tossed it into the fireplace. A bit of tobacco ash landed on the head of the cat. Thus rudely awakened from his nap, he looked up at Mr. Dunn, yowled at him, and trotted over to the table to stare at me. Mr. Dunn muttered a quick apology to the cat, who acknowledged it by hopping onto the table and sticking his nose into my glass of port.

"I think that's a bit rich for you," I said to the cat, interposing my arm between nose and glass. He backed away one step.

"Sailed with a ship's cat once who liked ale," Mr. Dunn said. "Didn't seem to hurt him any."

"Ale may be considered a foodstuff. Port is a luxury to which he doesn't need introduction."

"From that look he's giving you, I'd say he's already acquainted."

Since I'm not particularly adept at winning feline staring contests and wished to finish my glass in peace, I dabbed my finger in the port and offered it up. It was duly sniffed and licked.

"Not much chance of shooing him out now," Mr. Dunn said.

"As he's the one who adopted me, I don't know that I had much chance anyway."

"You think Cass will buy that argument?"

"I'm not sure. We've never much discussed the subject of house pets." The decision would really be Mrs. Jenner's. I thought we might persuade her that Mr. Lightner was under government orders to keep the cat, since he had followed me back from the Patent Office.

"At any rate, I'd rather not complicate the current situation with Madame Serurier," I said as I gave the cat another lick of port. "So Mr. Cat, you and Mr. Lightner will just have to find some basis for mutual acceptance."

Mr. Cat stretched himself, hopped off the table and onto the bed, circled around until he found the right spot on the counterpane, and began to wash. Cat for "I accept."

"He can hold his liquor," Mr. Dunn said.

"Perhaps he's a tavern cat grown weary of drunks stepping on his tail."

"I could ask around."

"I suspect we'll need your time for other things."

There was a knock at the door. It wasn't someone I particularly wanted to see.

"Mrs. Crofton! Mrs. Jenner didn't tell me … I'm terribly sorry, I didn't mean to intrude."

"Not at all, Dr. Thornton. I was just sharing a glass of port with a friend. Do come in." He took a few cautious steps into the room as I quickly closed the door behind him. The cat looked up but stayed put. Mr. Dunn came over and extended his hand.

"Hello, Doctor. It's been awhile."

"Mr. Dunn?"

"The same. Although I may look a shade darker to you than I did last year."

"No," Dr. Thornton said, shaking Mr. Dunn's hand. "You do look a little thinner."

"Didn't always eat regular after I left the navy."

"Yes, I understand there had been some reorganization of the gunboat commands. You weren't interested in a transfer?"

"I wasn't interested in a demotion."

Dr. Thornton nodded, but said nothing further. I'm sure he wanted to know what Mr. Dunn and I were doing by ourselves in Mr. Lightner's room, but since we were properly dressed and the bed neatly made, the obvious suspicions were blunted. I offered the wing chair and a glass of port.

"I'm sorry you had to leave yesterday's concert early, Doctor," I said. "The Gossec was well played."

"I'm sure it was."

"I believe Madame Serurier was quite pleased with the overall interpretation, although she did have some quarrel with the tempo taken in the middle section."

"I haven't had a chance to discuss it with her."

"You should. She was almost lukewarm in her praise."

"I'm glad to hear it."

"She thinks the Marine Band is capable of becoming one of our more enduring cultural institutions. Not yet to the standards of the Paris Conservatory, of course, but increasingly adequate. For an outpost such as Washington City, as she reminded us, that is no small achievement, and if only more French bandsmen could be recruited, well … but then, so many were misplaced on the road from Moscow."

"Mrs. Crofton …"

"I take it you need to speak with Mr. Lightner."

Dr. Thornton looked around the room before responding. His deliberateness suggested that he was calculating a salary adjustment for Mr. Lightner; whether upwards or downwards was difficult to ascertain.

"I wasn't aware that Mr. Lightner had a cat," he said.

"The cat wasn't either until this afternoon," I said.

"Rather distinctive markings. I think I've seen it before." He walked towards the bed for a closer look. I decided to adjust the counterpane and pillows before he got it.

"Or one very similar. Black and white with ginger striping is very popular in cats this season. Just ask Madame Serurier."

"Frankly, Mrs. Crofton, I'm not sure I care to trouble her for a few days."

"I know how you feel," Mr. Dunn said, prompting looks from both Dr. Thornton and me. "She's a hard woman to puzzle out. From what I recall."

"Anyway," Dr. Thornton said, "I have more urgent matters to deal with than music and fashion. Do you expect Mr. Lightner soon?"

"Any moment," I said. In fact, I had no idea, but I wanted to make sure Dr. Thornton didn't leave before revealing what was on his mind. I signaled to Mr. Dunn to stretch things out.

"He should have been back by now," Mr. Dunn said.

"Where from?" Dr. Thornton asked.

"Fishing trip."

"In today's weather?"

"Fish bite in fog as well as sunshine."

"Still not the wisest thing to do on one's own."

"That's why he asked me to row him. Figured I knew the river better."

"But you didn't go?"

"Oh, I went."

"And you left him somewhere on the river?"

"No."

"Then you brought him back."

"I did."

"Would you mind telling me where?"

"Not at all."

Dr. Thornton waited for Mr. Dunn to elaborate. Mr. Dunn waited for Dr. Thornton to ask another question. I knew that the next step in the ancient military art of frustrating one's superior was for either a junior officer to intervene or the superior to explode, so I opted to play junior officer.

"Mr. Dunn, I believe you mentioned that Mr. Lightner had some haggling to do over the boat rental."

"Oh, yeah, he did. Something about a leak and an overcharge."

"And he asked you to bring the fish here so that Mrs. Jenner could get to work on them right away."

"No point in risking spoilage over a few cents."

"If it were only a few cents," Dr. Thornton said, "I'm surprised he bothered."

"He's quite careful with his accounts," I said. "A habit no doubt acquired from the demands of his employment."

At which point the door swung open and Mr. Lightner stepped into the room. I suspect he'd been listening and waiting for a reasonable entrance line.

"Dr. Thornton, how good to see you, sir," he said. "An unexpected pleasure for a Sunday." Dr. Thornton got a handshake, Mr. Dunn got a clap on the shoulder and I got a peck on the cheek. Not a bad performance for a man who suspected his boss of murder.

"No greeting for the family pet?" Dr. Thornton asked. I cocked my head towards the bed. Mr. Lightner controlled his surprise, and gave the cat a quick scratch behind the ears. Luckily, the cat wasn't in a biting mood.

“I hope you were able to settle the matter of the overcharge to your satisfaction,” Dr. Thornton said.

“Overcharge?”

“On the leaky boat,” I said.

“A gross error, as I understand it,” Dr. Thornton said.

“Ah, yes, yes, I did. All taken care of. So you’ve been told about this morning’s trip?”

“Yes,” I said, “and I was just about to mention how lovely it was of you to brave all that inclemency just to secure a few trout for our dinner. Really, Dr. Thornton, there are times when I suppose I can be a trifle particular, but you must admit that the fish on offer at the Central Market aren’t always first quality. I’m sure Mrs. Thornton can attest to that.”

“She can and does.”

“But I would have to guess that you’re not here to discuss the inefficiencies in Washington City’s piscine distribution system, sir,” Mr. Lightner said.

“No, I’m not. May we speak privately?”

I started coughing.

“My apologies, Dr. Thornton. I must have taken a chill whilst walking over here. Dear me.” I produced a handkerchief and slumped into the wing chair. Mr. Dunn quickly echoed my coughs.

“It wouldn’t be right to send Mrs. Crofton and Mr. Dunn away from the fire, sir.”

“They were perfectly fine when I arrived a short while ago.”

“Dr. Thornton, as a physician, you of all people should recognize the signs of incendiary catarrh.”

“Never heard of it.”

“Good lord, sir, with all respect, it is mentioned by both Hippocrates and Galen, not to mention fully expounded by Paracelsus, who, if I recall correctly, theorized in detail on the rapidity of symptomatic onset. Maybe you know it by another name. You know how translations from the Latin can vary.”

"Mr. Lightner, I have neither time nor inclination to debate the veracity of your amateur medical knowledge. If you'll come with me to the office ..."

"Sir, I can't leave them in this condition."

Dr. Thornton gave each of us a stern look. Mr. Dunn and I increased the tempo and volume of our expectorations.

"Besides, sir, I think they've progressed to a state of blockage in the eustachian tubes."

Dr. Thornton shook his head and sighed. "Never mind. Have a look at this." He reached into his coat pocket and took out a piece of notepaper. It was wrapped around a slice of cheese.

"I believe you'll find both items self-explanatory. Now, if you'll excuse me, I have a dinner appointment with a couple of New York congressmen. They want me to evaluate their plans for an expanded courthouse in Buffalo. Personally, I don't think that canal they're talking about digging through to New York City has a prayer in hell, but I suspect Buffalo can use all the assistance I can give it. And if that cough doesn't clear up as soon as I'm out the door, tea infused with honey and lemon every three hours." He nodded to us and left.

"Incendiary catarrh," I said. "Nicely improvised. I'll have to remember that one."

"Yes, very well played, both of you," Mr. Lightner said. "Maybe you should consider taking up amateur dramatics with the Thespians."

"There's no need for you to be snippy about it."

"I don't care to look more foolish in front of Dr. Thornton than I have to."

"I didn't think you wanted to be left alone with him."

"That's beside the point."

"What does the note say?"

"Help yourself."

As Mr. Lightner helped himself to a glass of port, Mr. Dunn and I examined both note and cheese. The latter was undoubtedly kashkaval. The former was brief, the words rather sloppily composed from letters extracted from a newspaper.

"So kidnappers actually bother with this sort of thing," I said.

"I guess one would if one doesn't want you to recognize his handwriting," Mr. Lightner said.

"Well, if you're interested, this note gives the government a forty-eight hour deadline to ransom the cheese."

"Great." Mr. Lightner picked up the copy of the *National Intelligencer* sitting on the floor next to the wing chair.

"I doubt that the letters can all be matched to a single newspaper," I said.

"I'm looking at the shipping news. I want to see if there's a ship leaving for Spanish Florida by Tuesday."

"Cheer up, Cass," Mr. Dunn said. "At least we can eliminate Dr. Thornton."

"Why? It would be just like him to write himself a ransom note and deliver it personally to put me off the scent."

"I think you are now being more than a little imaginative, my love."

"Whatever you say. Charlie, what'd you find in Brackenridge's room?"

"A few letters, like Madeleine told us. Not much to them."

"I spent two hours fending off the advances of a drunken hotel clerk for nothing?"

"There was one about a Turkish high something-or-other that neither of them liked."

"Hold on," Mr. Lightner said. "That's significant. She and Brackenridge must have known each other when he was a diplomat."

"Or they each knew the official at different times," I said.

"Show me the letter, Charlie."

"I didn't bring it."

"Why the hell not?"

"Why the hell do you think?"

The mutually raised voices woke the cat, which let out a sharp cry of reproach and proceeded to stare Mr. Lightner down. Mr. Lightner apologized to the cat before turning back to Mr. Dunn. "Did the letter indicate one way or the other?"

"No. It was just remember old so-and-so with the big ears and the squeaky voice."

"That describes any number of eunuchs in the Sultan's government," I said. "I doubt we have time to cross-reference them."

"What about the other letters?"

"One of them read like a pamphlet on the great cheeses of Europe. Mostly France."

"Nothing surprising there," I said.

"There was a third where she commented on Brackenridge's sheep farming. Something about an uncle who wintered over with a Basque shepherd to refine his technique."

"And that's it?"

"That's what I recall."

Mr. Lightner paced for a bit in front of the fireplace. "Diplomats know how to use invisible ink."

Mr. Dunn and I shook our heads.

"Well, all right," Mr. Lightner said. "Today, she was waiting to give him some friendly advice. We'll assume it's pertinent to his business. What does that suggest?"

"Perhaps she's considering an investment," I said.

"Which would eliminate her as the cheese thief," Charlie said.

"Why?" Mr. Lightner said. "What if she didn't get the deal she wanted? What better way to put pressure on Brackenridge?"

"Cassius, if she's looking to play a major role in the birth of industrial cheese-making, why would she slice up the very item intended to launch that industry? And even if she did, why send the slice and the note to Dr. Thornton?"

"Maybe she didn't. Maybe she sent it to Brackenridge because he missed their meeting, and he gave it to Dr. Thornton."

"In one afternoon?"

"Possible, if the cheese is now being hidden near McKeowin's. She rows back, cuts out the slice …"

"Cuts up several newspapers which she happens to have stored for the occasion along with a pot of paste, veils herself, walks over to the hotel, drops the parcel at the desk, and walks away without anyone noticing. Then, Mr. Brackenridge returns, just happens to see that the parcel on the desk is addressed to him, and hurries it over to the Thornton house in time for Dr. Thornton to bring it here without missing his dinner appointment. All this without either Madame or Mr. Brackenridge bumping into either of you. Possible, perhaps. Plausible, no."

"Especially seeing as how Brackenridge ain't exactly built for speed," Mr. Dunn said.

"I still think she's involved in the disappearance of the cheese," Mr. Lightner said. "Why else would she demand to meet Brackenridge on Mason's Island?"

"Then who left the ransom note for Dr. Thornton?" I asked.

"Whoever she's involved with."

I frowned at the simplicity of the logic. "On her instructions?"

"Sure."

"Cousin Ray," Mr. Dunn said.

"Assuming he can read and paste," I said.

"He's the only person besides Coleman and Brackenridge who knew where the cheese was. She provides the brains and the political know-how. He provides the muscle. And Coleman sure acted like he'd been double-crossed."

"You're suggesting that Madeline Serurier is blackmailing both the federal government and Samuel Brackenridge at the same time," I said. "That's a dangerous game even for her."

"She does like to hedge her bets. Like wearing extra stockings when playing strip whist." This elicited raised eyebrows from Mr. Lightner, at which Mr. Dunn grinned and shrugged. I made a mental note to teach Mr. Lightner the nuances of the game once his mind was cleared of both missing cheese and unavenged murder.

"I think Amanda may have a point, though," Mr. Lightner said. "Hedging bets is one thing, upping the ante another."

"Still, if Cousin Ray's anything like Coleman, I can't see him as the mastermind," Mr. Dunn said.

"He may not be. Coleman didn't think Cousin Ray patched the barn wall. He had to be working with someone else."

"So she hired Ray, and Ray hired a friend. Not likely the friend was in charge in that case."

"Then maybe Cousin Ray double-crossed her, too. And if he's not the brains, and the friend isn't, who's he working for? Which brings me back to Dr. Thornton. He sets me after the cheese to deflect suspicion from him, and the second note's just part of that process. Amanda, did you find anything in his desk?"

"Sketches."

"Of?"

"Platforms. Gears. Nothing to suggest kidnapping and murder, unless he was working on a new form of rack."

"But that's it, isn't it? Potential conflicts of interest. Suppose he's developing a competing cheese press. He stalls the approval of Brackenridge's patent until he can find a way to substitute his own that doesn't reek. Madame's blackmail plot provides the opportunity."

"You're assuming he found out about the cousins," I said. "And that Brackenridge lied about where he sent the cheese because he was suspicious of Dr. Thornton."

"Plausible on both counts. So then Walter finds something incriminating, and Dr. Thornton kills him—or has him killed. Madame guesses this, and tests it at the concert."

"Because?" I asked.

"Because ... because this whole thing is one of their argument games which has gotten lethally out of hand!" He flung himself on the bed, narrowly missing the cat, who bounded off the bed and onto the seat of the wing chair.

"And would you mind explaining that?" Mr. Lightner asked.

"Felinus domesticus," I replied. "I believe the medicinal effects of its companionship were noted by both Hippocrates and Galen."

"And fully expounded by Paracelsus," Mr. Dunn said.

The cat curled himself deep into the chair. If he had a theory about the cheese-napping and the murder, he wasn't saying.

19

"And those three stars, they make up Orion's belt. You have to fill in the sword that hangs from it."

Mr. Cat didn't seem particularly impressed, though he did seem to be paying attention. Reminded me of boyhood nights I spent sitting on the back of a wagon with my father, more or less listening to his tours of the heavens. "Cass, you need to know what Mr. Shakespeare was thinking when he refers to this star or that. If you imagine it clearly, so does your audience." Slightly ahead of most of his contemporaries is my father, which may account for why he's achieved only a middling success. But then, at my current rate of progress, I wasn't even going to get within semaphore range of middling. I now had only thirty-eight hours out of the second note's deadline—faked by Dr. Thornton or not—and I still had no idea where to find hard evidence of anyone's plotting. Which is why I was up at an ungodly hour giving an astronomy lesson to a cat.

When the cat began his insistent scratching at the door, Charlie refused to let it disturb his sleep. I'd have turned to Amanda, but with Charlie avoiding Madame, Amanda was back at the French Ministry. So the cat and I tiptoed our way down the back stairs and onto the porch, where I sat for a few minutes waiting for him to take off into the early morning dark. Curiously he didn't. The stars were as good a way as any to clear my head.

"Well, we've done the zodiac, the dippers, and the hunter. Speaking of which, maybe it's time for you to chase down a rodent or two. Might be easier to explain you to Mrs. Jenner if you reduce the threat to her vegetable garden."

Mr. Cat stretched out his front paws, but only to make himself more comfortable.

"You'll have to make yourself useful at some point. I'm going to be hard-pressed to replicate that nice bit of Virginia ham you had for supper. Not to mention the port."

He yawned.

"Seriously, if you're looking for a long-term berth, you were right the first time. Amanda's the rich widow. At least comfortable. More than I am. She keeps telling me she doesn't mind, but if she doesn't, why is she so keen to improve my prospects?"

Head down on the paws, eyes half shut. Well, I don't suppose I could have expected more of a response. He'd known us for less than a day. And he probably sensed that the question was largely rhetorical.

"So why don't you run along to the French Ministry? I guarantee you they've plenty of tidbits you'd find of interest, even if you don't like garlic. Come on, I'll head you in the right direction." Sure enough, as I stood up, Mr. Cat did likewise. We both stretched then headed to the front yard gate. Mrs. Jenner really needs to keep that oiled. Luckily, it didn't wake her, and we proceeded down a deserted F Street without having to answer awkward questions. The day's fog hadn't fully dissipated, and with only a quarter-moon's light filtering through to silhouette the houses scattered along the block, I slowed my usual quick pace. Mr. Cat trotted steadily alongside. It was his time of the morning, not mine.

Four blocks down to 15th, and he stopped just short of the old Rhodes Tavern.

"Sorry, friend. If you hadn't been this way for awhile, it's become a bank. No late parties to sniff out. You may as well continue on to the ministry."

Mr. Cat eased onto his haunches and looked up at me.

"It's only four more blocks, then a half block right to E. You don't really need me to escort you."

He stood still.

"Look, my night vision's worse than yours. If I take you all the way, I seriously increase my risk of stumbling and breaking some part of my anatomy."

He yowled. Twice.

"All right, all right, no need to make someone think we're trying to rob the place. Come on."

I walked ahead. About ten paces, and another yowl. Mr. Cat hadn't budged. I walked back to him.

"I'm not carrying you. Let's go."

Ten paces, another yowl.

"Suit yourself. I'm going home."

Ten paces back towards 11th, another yowl.

"Now what?"

We stood and watched each other for a few moments. I wondered about the significance of ten paces. Maybe I'd violated some territorial boundary and Mr. Cat found himself obligated to challenge me to a duel. It would hardly be a fair fight—his claws were sharper than mine. True, there wasn't anyone around to see me run from a cat, but still …

He ambled over and rubbed up against my legs. Okay, I hadn't offended him. But when I reached down to pet him, he trotted back to his spot, paused, then turned right towards E Street. This time, he went ten paces. Two glowing eyes floating above four white paws. Very spooky.

Turn back and listen to Charlie snore, or follow?

I walked slowly towards the eyes and paws. The rest of Mr. Cat reappeared, led me to the corner of E, and turned right again.

He was taking me to the Patent Office.

Maybe he wanted help with his bags.

20

"Mrs. Woodley, she looks absolutely ghastly. You must get her proper medical attention. Immediately."

"I'm afraid you don't understand, Mrs. Crofton. There's nothing more I can do."

"Well, there's nothing I can do. She's beyond the scope of my expertise."

What I did know was that Anne Frederick was dying. I was sure that Mrs. Woodley knew that as well, but she was making every effort to deny it.

"I do take care of my girls, Mrs. Crofton. The reputation of this house depends on that."

The sounds of someone packing her possessions into a trunk belied that proposition as they echoed down into the empty parlor below. Mrs. Woodley stood at the foot of the stairs looking up towards her room, and I'd almost reached the front door. But I had been asked to help, and I couldn't simply walk out, even if the only thing left was to make a futile appeal to Mrs. Woodley's conscience.

"And you think that evicting a dying woman enhances that reputation?"

Her business conscience, of course. I'm sure that whatever other sentiments of which she's capable aren't overly lavished on her employees.

"Mrs. Crofton, the house has only a limited amount of, shall we say, work space. As a woman interested in business yourself, surely you understand that I can't take an entire room out of profit for very long."

"If you're looking for absolution, Mrs. Woodley, that is also beyond the scope of my expertise."

Rather than answer, Mrs. Woodley excused herself, charged upstairs, and engaged herself in an agitated colloquy with the maid who was attending to the contents of Anne's trunk. I couldn't tell whether her concern was time or theft. In that house, probably both.

"Hannah's been with me a long time, and I do trust her as much as you can trust a housemaid," Mrs. Woodley said after she trotted back down the stairs. "But there are times when she is infuriatingly slow to task."

"Perhaps she's not keen on evicting Miss Frederick."

"No concern whether she is or she isn't. My morning clients will arrive soon, and I don't need her dawdling over every peculiar keepsake that girl owns."

It wasn't one of my better impulses, but the sudden pang of jealousy I felt forced me to inquire.

"Would we be talking about something given by a favorite client?"

Mrs. Woodley smiled at me for the first time since my arrival. I'd given her some leverage.

"I don't know, Mrs. Crofton. I don't keep track of personal gifts."

I was sure she had them all catalogued with names, dates, and estimated values, but my desire for knowledge precluded arguing the point.

"However, it's not unusual for my girls to receive the occasional token in the course of regular visitation. Given for the performance of some particularly satisfying service. Or peculiarly satisfying service, as the case may be."

I'm sure my face was growing redder by the moment as disquieting images began to invade my thoughts. I was determined to keep my composure, but like it or not, I had been hooked.

"To what sort of peculiar services do you refer, Mrs. Woodley?"

Mrs. Woodley shouted at Hannah to finish up, to which Hannah mumbled some obsequiousness or other. No doubt she added an unflattering gesture or two when Mrs. Woodley turned her attention back to me.

"Now, Mrs. Crofton, a lady like you shouldn't be concerned with such things. She might well find them upsetting."

"I am a daughter of His Majesty's Royal Navy, Mrs. Woodley. There are few peculiarities of human conduct with which I have not been acquainted."

"Personally?"

I took a deep breath. "Not personally."

"Pity. I always welcome the opportunity to exchange ideas."

Mrs. Woodley waited for me to respond. My teeth edged their way into my lower lip to keep me from doing so.

"Now, that favorite client you mentioned, let me see … I don't recall hearing about anything distasteful."

I released some of the pressure on my lip.

"But then, what's distasteful to one lady is just sport for another," she said.

Did my fiancé have dark impulses that he struggled to keep from me? More to the point, was he having a bit of fun on which I was missing out?

"Mrs. Woodley, I understand that you employ in this house a certain book."

"You know about the bible?"

"I don't believe it's a terribly well-kept secret."

"Well, it wouldn't be, would it? These things do tend to attract attention."

"And since only a select group of individuals have ever seen it, a good deal of speculation as to its contents."

"Foolish gossip, that's all that is. There's nothing in it that you won't find in most any decent house in Washington City."

"Really? I thought the book was exclusive to this house."

"Not exclusive, no. Rare, yes. I don't think there's more than another two or three original King Jameses in the whole region."

Mrs. Woodley was going to give me neither a straight answer nor a peek without a trade. And when Hannah appeared at the top of the stairs with the grand announcement that she'd just about finished packing, I had to make one.

"Mrs. Woodley, it's not the King James in which I'm interested."

"I see. Well, that is the house bible."

"The volume to which I refer is more in the nature of an operations manual."

"Ah. You mean the playbook."

"I'd be most curious to see it."

"I'm sure you would. And no doubt you'd like me to point out which little plays might have appealed to a certain favorite client. Prompting a gift or two."

"It would be a favor for which I'd be quite grateful."

"Grateful enough to see to Anne?"

I drew another deep breath. "The ladies of the Washington City Orphan Asylum Society might be persuaded to find a place for Miss Frederick," I said. "Provided, of course, that she is, indeed, an orphan."

"Oh, I can assure you of that. She has no family at all. Something about an accident with a runaway. A coach or a wagon, I'd guess; she never did say exactly."

"And you never did press her for the details."

"I never do."

"May I see the book?"

Mrs. Woodley beckoned me into her office, unlocked a drawer in her desk, and took out a large, nicely gilded black leather folio.

"I'll see what's keeping that maid," she said.

The book contained not only the little plays, but a log chronicling the particulars of each occasion on which a given play had been requested, cross-filed to the young lady requested to act it out. Good business practice, that. I turned to Anne's pages, and there, of course, was the most recent entry concerning the city marshal's frolic as a milkmaid on the night of Mr. Dunn's arrest.

The marshal had incapacitated Mr. Dunn with a most curious object.

An object he shouldn't have found.

The same object Hannah couldn't quite fit into Anne's trunk.

21

"Charlie, put out the pipe."

"I'm not wearin' the footman's coat. I can smoke."

"You're a military man. You know damn well not to signal an ambush."

"Ambush ain't usually a concern in a boat with a big white sail and a cannon sticking out the bow."

"I don't want to give him a chance to lock us out."

"Then maybe I should go down to Central Market and tell some of the women there's a sale on."

"Do me the favor, okay?"

Charlie took a few more puffs, then slowly put away his pipe.

"Damn cat," he said. "Too nosy for our own good."

"Stop complaining. I was the one who had to dig the things up."

No, I hadn't relished standing behind the Patent Office in the middle of the night and working my hands through a compost heap studded with odd lengths of splintered lumber. But the boots were stuck, and somehow Mr. Cat figured I was the man for the job. And when I ran the leather through my fingers, there it was, like Amanda had drawn: four little leaves surrounded by a thin line, repeating in a band around the edge.

Flecked with blood.

"So tell me again," Charlie said, "how much force can I use on Walker to keep him from yelling for the marshal?"

"I'm sure we can do this in a civilized manner."

"Uh huh. He gets jumped by two men on his way to open his store and his first instinct is to get us all a cup of tea."

"Well, then, since he's seen you before, maybe you should approach him first."

"Being on my own and out of uniform might just make him suspicious."

"All right, I'll approach him first. You stay out of sight until I've got him to open the door."

"How about that rain barrel over there? You want me to see if I fit inside?"

"Just watch my back."

"I will. He pulls a dancing pump on you, I'll be there."

I frowned at Charlie and looked at my pocket watch. A few more minutes. Charlie wasn't buying my idea that S. Dunham Walker might be Walter's killer, and having met the man, maybe he had a point. But then he'd suggested that the murderer might be female, and if that were possible, I didn't see why the effeminate Mr. Walker wouldn't qualify. Clearly, the red Moroccans came from his shop. It was a new shop. Maybe he figured to help his cash flow by hiring himself out as an assassin.

Well, maybe. But at this point even a fanciful theory merited pursuit. And since a store full of shoeboxes is a store full of blunt objects, I didn't want to take more chances than necessary.

"There's your man," Charlie said.

S. Dunham Walker hurried around a corner onto Pennsylvania, loose blond hair and loose red coat flying about. Short, thin, and heading towards us with a gait that suggested a scurrying mouse, I had to admit that he didn't appear to be much of a threat.

"So you sure you can take him alone?" Charlie asked.

"How do you know he doesn't carry a big folding knife in his pocket?"

"If he does, it's got a pearl handle and the bloodiest thing it's been poked into is a watermelon."

So why did I still feel jittery? I hailed Walker as he unlocked his door.

"I'm terribly sorry, sir," Walker said, "but I don't commence business for another half hour."

"That's fine, Mr. Walker. I'm not interested in buying a pair of shoes this morning."

The look on Walker's face changed quickly from irritation to fear. I stopped him before he screamed for help.

"Lightner. State Department. Office of Procurement."

"Oh!" Walker's fear changed to embarrassment. Yes, I'd instinctively played the same card as I had with Tom Coleman, and I suppose I could have been more imaginative. But federal money, like a bawdy comedy, is always a crowd pleaser.

"I'm thinking about buying quite a few pairs of shoes," I said. "That's why I thought it best to discuss the matter in the absence of other customers."

"Well, then, please, please come in. Take a chair. If you'll just allow me a moment to settle myself, I'll be more than happy to see what I can do for you."

In his excitement over the prospect of a government contract, Walker neglected to lock the door behind us, so as he bustled himself through the curtain behind the store counter, I let Charlie in as quietly as I could. Charlie leaned himself against the door as I sat down. Walker registered his surprise as he bustled back into the sales room.

"Mr. Dunn here consults for our department," I said. "He's an expert in leather goods."

"Is he? But, and forgive me if I'm mistaken, Mr. Lightner, this man was in here not a week ago, and I distinctly remember him as a mere servant. To an English lady. Rather a fussy lady, if I may say."

Charlie and I restrained ourselves.

"Ah, yes, you see that would have been standard procedure," I said.

"To dress an expert as a servant?"

"Exactly. Mr. Walker, I can already see from the shoes you have on display that you're a merchant of particular sensibility to fine quality leatherwork."

"I will not deal in anything flimsy. That's why I order from the better Philadelphia boot makers."

"As you advertise. But, and forgive me if I'm mistaken, there are other merchants in footwear who would have no qualms about advertising the same and yet delivering merchandise made by some backwoods cobblers in New Jersey or Delaware."

"Oh, if only we could eliminate them from the business! Simply wipe them off the footwear map!" He flared his nostrils and punched his hand. Suddenly, I visualized him swinging a crutch.

"Yes, well, those of us in my office are encouraged to use more subtle methods to protect the public. Thus I sent Mr. Dunn around in a capacity in which he would not arouse any particular attention."

"To inspect my stock?"

"And you didn't even notice I was doing it," Charlie said.

"But that's no reflection on you, Mr. Walker," I said. "Mr. Dunn's one of our most adept agents."

"Then the English lady ... But I didn't think the federal service employed women."

"She's a talented amateur who lends us a hand from time to time."

Walker sat down and thought for a moment. "So you sent your team to evaluate my fitness to become a government supplier."

"You are new to the District. And we do have to spend the taxpayer's money with utmost care."

Walker nodded while Charlie tried not to laugh.

"And may I presume that your visit indicates that my fitness has been found acceptable?" Walker asked.

"My visit constitutes phase two of our evaluation process," I said.

"Phase two? How many phases are there?"

"I'm afraid I can't specify that."

"Oh." Walker looked crestfallen. "Mr. Lightner, I don't mean to appear rude, but if we are involved in a lengthy process, perhaps you could return at a time when I could give you my fullest attention. I do have to ready the shop for opening."

"Mr. Walker, are you familiar with the current situation in Spanish Florida?"

"Mr. Lightner, I really must ask ..."

"Maybe you should be. General Jackson certainly is."

"General Jackson?"

"Hero of New Orleans," Charlie said.

"Yes, I know who he is," Walker snapped, though he didn't exhibit any signs of nervousness like Randolph had when I'd asked him if he'd met Samuel Brackenridge. Maybe Walker had no connection with the cheese-napping. "In fact, I'm planning to send him a personal invitation to visit my shop when he arrives here next month."

"Are you?" I said. "Then it's all the more imperative that we complete phase two immediately."

"Do you mean that General Jackson has something to do with my evaluation?"

"All I can say is that the General has a keen interest in the substance of the particular contract that may be at issue."

"Very keen," Charlie said. "Very keen on the quality of the leather. In his experience, the Louisiana swamps and the Florida swamps ..."

"Mr. Dunn, I'm afraid you may have already divulged too much," I said.

Walker leaned forward. "Mr. Lightner, are we talking about supplying a military expedition?"

"I'm not at liberty to confirm that."

"Oh, but you're not denying it, either." Walker shot up from his chair and hurried back through the curtain. I knew all too well the sound that followed: the rasp of shoebox scraping against shoebox. Walker returned with an open box.

"Mr. Dunn, you've already examined the ladies' version, so you must agree that these are absolutely perfect for General Jackson."

"They are some of the best Moroccan boots I've ever seen," Charlie said.

"You know, gentlemen, when I first looked at the samples, I knew that red would please the ladies, yet I couldn't be certain about it as a man's color. After all, they are a marked departure from your chestnuts and cordovans and such, not to mention very, shall we say, flamboyant in relation to the traditional black. But, of course! It's a hero's color. Just like a Spartan battle cloak!"

I stopped visualizing him swinging a crutch.

"Mr. Walker," I said, "if the State Department were to consider these boots suitable for General Jackson's consideration ..."

"They are, Mr. Lightner, they most positively are. Surely you can see that they can be for no one else."

"And thus, perhaps, gain the general's approval for a further inquiry into the appropriate specifications for the more rank-and-file footwear ..."

"I assure you, sir, one fitting and he will feel like King Leonidas himself."

"We would have to be in a position to certify to the general the uniqueness of these boots."

"We are, we are. These are the only pair in the District."

"The only men's pair," Charlie said.

"As I said, I knew that red would please the ladies, so naturally I ordered several pair for them. The men's I had made up on a trial basis, and I've been holding them, as it were, in reserve."

"That's all well and good, Mr. Walker, " I said, "but General Jackson would hardly feel like King Leonidas if he were to pick up a newspaper and discover that his special boots were also the latest fashion in Baltimore, Philadelphia, and New York."

"That couldn't happen. I have a special arrangement with the maker. The trial of the men's version is exclusive to me."

"Then if that's the case, I must ask you to halt any sales of the ladies' version."

"But ..."

"Until we've presented the men's to the general. Once he's given his endorsement, I'd be surprised if you wouldn't have to greatly expand your delivery capacity in order to satisfy the demands of his female admirers."

Walker's eyes widened.

"That and a federal contract for military supply … well!" he said.

"And, of course, I will need the names of those ladies to whom you've already sold boots."

"May I ask for what purpose?"

"A direct survey of customer satisfaction."

"But Mr. Dunn has already certified the quality."

"Quality to the hand and eye is one thing," Charlie said. "Obviously, I can't say how they feel on the foot. Especially after a few days."

"Which would be a minimal criterion when what General Jackson has in mind might involve a considerable amount of marching," I said.

"I … well, Mr. Lightner, I do want to cooperate with my government."

"I knew you were a patriotic man."

"Only …"

"Only what? Surely you maintain accurate sales records."

"Yes, of course. It's only that …"

"Mr. Walker, as you've already noted, the general will arrive here next month. He will expect to see a list of properly vetted potential suppliers. In order to move promptly to the next phase of your evaluation, I must have those names."

Walker paced and wrung his hands.

"Mr. Lightner, I have sold a pair, but in the strictest confidence."

"I don't understand. A woman who buys a pair of these boots would certainly want to show them off."

"I agree. But this particular customer insisted that the transaction remain private."

"Why?"

"I don't know. It wasn't my place to ask."

I headed for the door. “Our evaluation will have to take that into account. Pity. All those feet needing protection from all those swamps.”

“Snakes, crocodiles,” Charlie added. “Could be the general demands more than one kind of boot. Could double or triple the size of the contract.”

“Mr. Lightner, please! I can’t breach a confidence. It could ruin my business.”

“Mr. Walker, we must follow procedure. The integrity of the civil service depends on it. However, I’m not unsympathetic to your situation. I may be able to interpret certain procedures in certain ways. But I have to have some information to go on. A description of the woman at the least.”

“I’m sorry, but it’s simply not possible for me to do that.”

I glanced at Charlie, who flexed his knuckles. Reluctantly, I shook my head at him.

“Then give us a hint,” I said to Walker. “A suggestion on which we might base further investigation. The party in question could hardly complain about your conduct if any revelations resulted from an independent investigation.”

“No, no, the party couldn’t. I can see that. In that case, the party shouldn’t have any complaint against me at all.”

“So what can you tell us?”

Nothing that made Charlie and I feel any better about who stole the cheese and killed Walter.

22

"Cassius, she did not kill Walter Clarkson."

"Who else? Who else would have had the red boots?"

"Kindly keep your voice down."

"Why? Is Walter going to tell someone?"

"The kitchen staff might."

Mr. Lightner made a grumbling noise at me and strode over to re-check the lock on the cellar door. He didn't yet know that I'd just settled Anne into bed in my room, and I didn't yet know that I wanted him to, figuring that he'd be busy enough to avoid Mrs. Woodley's until I decided how and when to tell him.

"So you'd say it was another wife in the diplomatic corps?" Mr. Dunn asked. He was much calmer than Mr. Lightner, but then I'd authorized him to open one of the Seruriers' lesser Bordeaux to help us parse things out.

"I'd say that Mr. Walker's use of the words 'gift' and 'diplomatic service' wasn't conclusive proof that Madeleine Serurier was either purchaser or recipient."

"And you think the blood on the boots was what?" Mr. Lightner said. "Evidence of a squirrel fight?"

"It is possible that the blood isn't Mr. Clarkson's."

"Probable?"

"Probable as in why would this particular pair of boots with this particular design turns up under a pile of debris behind the Patent Office a week after Walter Clarkson thought he was being followed by someone? Perhaps not. But if they were Madame's, it's highly unlikely that she'd have committed to wearing them outdoors before breaking them in within the privacy of the house."

"But not impossible."

"Cassius, you're being difficult."

"I am not being difficult! I'm trying not to waste time by artfully reasoning around the obvious."

"Oh, is that what I'm doing? Well, then, if you no longer value my participation, there are other things to which my artful reasoning can be better directed."

"Mrs. Crofton, I value your participation."

"Thank you, Mr. Dunn."

"I get much better drinks from you than from Cass." And he flashed me one of his 'you couldn't be angry with me even if you tried real hard' grins. I couldn't, and it did help blunt my irritation.

"Amanda, look at the connections here," Mr. Lightner said. "The Arabian design is on both the boots and Randolph's portfolio. Randolph seems to be hiding something about his relationship to Brackenridge. Madeleine seems to be hiding something about her relationship to Brackenridge. The boots were buried beneath Dr. Thornton's office window, which happens to be where Walter first got wind of the cheese-napping. And at Saturday's concert, Madeleine angers Dr. Thornton with hints about Walter's murder, then coyly tells us she thinks he's hiding something!"

"Back up a minute, Cass," Mr. Dunn said. "Sounds like you're saying that Brackenridge bought the boots for Madeleine."

Mr. Lightner smiled and clapped Mr. Dunn on the shoulder. "Charlie, that's exactly what I'm saying. Just like he must have bought the portfolio for Randolph. If he favors that particular design, it makes sense."

"Then you think her relationship with Brackenridge is, well, real personal?"

Mr. Lightner hesitated before answering. His logic had backed him into two possibilities. As to the first, I didn't think that Samuel Brackenridge had the energy to simultaneously court Mr. Randolph and Madame, even if he had the inclination.

"People give elaborate business gifts, too, Charlie."

That seemed the more reasonable possibility, even if I wasn't yet convinced.

"'Course, if she killed Walter, I don't guess I should fret much. But when you're playing games with a married woman – even a high-class French one – you do like to think you're the only player."

"Mr. Dunn," I said, "if Madame Serurier were playing games with Mr. Brackenridge, it hardly seems likely that she would have orchestrated the kidnapping of his prize cheese."

"Unless it was revenge," he said.

"Precisely. And if it were revenge, then the games were finished before you and she struck up your friendship."

"Guess that would be about right," he said, leaning back and taking a swig of the Bordeaux. Interesting how little it often takes to make a man feel good about a woman.

"Well done, Amanda," Mr. Lightner said. "You've just supplied the motive for the crimes. Clean and simple. Old as Greek tragedy. Woman scorned."

"Not necessarily."

"Why not?"

"Suppose she'd been scorned by someone other than Samuel Brackenridge."

"You mean Dr. Thornton? But we know they're not romantically involved."

"We know that she craves his attention. Even more, she craves his acknowledgement of her as a worthy intellectual and business partner."

"What she doesn't get from Louis Serurier."

"Essentially."

Mr. Dunn looked up from the bottle of Bordeaux. "Or me."

"Maybe Brackenridge can't give her the kind of personal attention that Dr. Thornton can, but maybe he supplies the business respect that Dr. Thornton won't," I said. "If she could maintain the two – and Louis Serurier might just allow her enough leeway to do so -- her world would be very nicely balanced."

"But Dr. Thornton is still stingy enough with his attentions to frustrate her," Mr. Lightner said, "and so that balance is maddeningly out of reach."

"From his point of view, a woman as forceful as Madame is both fascinating and frightening. And I suspect his conventional devotions to Mrs. Thornton get in the way. So to get a bit of hers back, at the concert, she plants suspicions about him being involved in Walter Clarkson's killing. That makes her a perverse practical joker, but not a murderess."

"Then maybe the best theory is what I suggested yesterday: she's blackmailing Brackenridge because he refused to cut her as good a deal as she wanted. And when Walter found out and threatened to blackmail her, she killed him."

"Cassius, she was eating dinner with us when he was killed."

"We don't really know when Walter was killed. Charlie and I didn't return until after dark. And when we did, you came down from your room. So she could have killed him before dinner."

"I don't recall hearing anything unusual."

"Did you have your windows open?"

"It was chilly. Most likely not."

Mr. Lightner began to pace around the whiskey barrels, playing the barrister. He appeared to be enjoying himself—shame I can't yet persuade him to take up the profession in earnest.

"Brackenridge gives her the boots," he said. "She tries them on. Decides to take a walk in the garden. Sees Walter. They have words."

"Even with the windows closed, Amanda would have heard a fight in the garden," Mr. Dunn said.

"They're both aware of that, so they whisper. Walter dismisses her. She walks away in a huff. He decides to use the privy. Determined to have the last word, she turns back. She sees the crutch, and ambushes him as he comes out."

"And then later that night she sneaks over to Blodgett's and buries the boots," Mr. Dunn said. He was also enjoying himself. Shame a black man can't become a barrister's clerk.

"Gentlemen, if I may draw your attention to the obvious, no one of consequence in Washington City would really believe that Dr. Thornton wears ladies' boots. At least not a pair too small for his feet. So if you're implying that Madame buried them behind the Patent Office to further implicate him in the murder, you're showing a pronounced disrespect for her common sense."

"If Dr. Thornton is involved in the cheese-napping, it makes sense as a private message," Mr. Lightner said. "A warning."

"You're grasping at straws."

"We don't have a better suspect."

I didn't reply immediately. I hated to admit that he was right, but it was looking that way. Neither Madame nor another diplomat's wife would have bought Anne Frederick the boots, so she was unlikely to have been Clarkson's killer. As for the city marshal? His penchant for garish cross-dressing might have involved a gift of female boots, but I doubted he'd have risked his reputation by wearing them outside Mrs. Woodley's or other private quarters. Both might still have been connected with the theft of the cheese, but I had no further support for that. Yet I just wasn't ready to accuse Madeleine Serurier.

"What we don't have is credible evidence," I said.

"And we're running out of time. We need to confront her as soon as she gets back."

"No! I'm going to have enough trouble explaining why there's a comatose prostitute lying on my bed. I don't need to complicate the situation with half-baked accusations!"

"What was that?"

"What was what?"

"About the prostitute."

Of the many reasons why we English are trained to remain calm in the midst of confrontation, information control is high on the list. I grabbed the Bordeaux from Mr. Dunn and took a swig.

"Amanda, I don't believe I've ever seen you drink without a proper glass," Mr. Lightner said.

"Yes, well, I didn't wish to appear rude by bolting upstairs to get one." I passed the bottle back to Mr. Dunn.

"Fine," Mr. Lightner said. "Now why is there a prostitute in your room?"

"Because she was thrown out of her house. And no, I don't indulge in young women behind your back. And yes, the woman is Anne Frederick."

Mr. Dunn let out a long whistle. Mr. Lightner managed the word "Anne."

"Petite young woman, auburn hair. Up the central staircase, turn left at the painting of the three nude graces, second room down." The realization that I'd set foot in Mrs. Woodley's stunned Mr. Lightner even more than finding out that Anne was here. He sat next to Mr. Dunn, who held out the Bordeaux. Mr. Lightner took a good swallow.

"Comatose?" he said.

"Virtually unresponsive. To her credit, Mrs. Woodley didn't feel she was up to earning her keep, although I imagine the patrons list contains a few men who'd pay well for that sort of thing."

"Each house has its limits," Mr. Dunn said.

"I saw her the night we found Walter's body," Mr. Lightner said. "Mrs. Woodley told me she'd stopped eating. But there weren't any other signs of disease. And she was talking."

"What about?" I asked.

"Apples."

"Are you sure?"

"Yes, I'm sure."

"Anything in particular about them?"

"Nothing that made any particular sense. She kept going on about a favorite of Thomas Jefferson's. German name, had a 'berg' in it."

"Spitzenberg."

"That's it. How'd you know?"

"Auntie Clarisse. The one who married the orchard magnate from Dorset."

"Sounds to me like a brain fever," Mr. Dunn said. "I've seen guys in sick bay with that. Talk all kinds of nonsense."

"Yeah, but she wasn't delirious, Charlie."

"Well, then, she was trying to explain something," I said. "What else do you remember?"

"Cider. Making cider. How making it with the Spitzenberg wasn't easy."

"That's sounds perfectly rational."

"And that it was dangerous. That didn't."

"I don't recall any warnings from Auntie Clarisse."

"Maybe Anne wasn't talking about the juice," Mr. Dunn said.

"Something poisonous to give the cider an extra kick?" Mr. Lightner said.

"No, the machinery. Maybe that kind of apple messes up the cider press."

"Of course!" I said.

"Of course what?" Mr. Lightner said.

I crouched my way over to a group of small casks stuck into a crawl space in the cellar's back wall, and removed that object of Anne's that wouldn't fit into her trunk. I handed it to Mr. Dunn.

"What do you make of this?"

"Crude. Roughly whittled tree branch. Maybe some kind of handle for something," Mr. Dunn said.

"Yes, I think so, too. A handle for a cider press?"

"Could be. More likely a quick replacement for the original."

"Where'd you get that?" Mr. Lightner asked.

"It belongs to Anne Frederick. I didn't want anyone to find it until I'd figured it out."

"Odd keepsake," Mr. Lightner said.

"Then you've never seen it?"

"No."

"Good. I suspected it wasn't one of her props. Nonetheless, the city marshal used it to knock out Mr. Dunn."

"Well, I'll be damned," Mr. Dunn said. "But I can't help you there. Didn't see what hit me."

"How do you know this was used on Charlie?"

"Surely, Cassius, you're aware of how meticulous Mrs. Woodley is about recording the result of each scenario played out by her girls."

"Actually, I wasn't."

"I imagine she does so to measure customer satisfaction. Give her suggestions for improvement. At any rate, on the night that Mr. Dunn paid his visit, the city marshal was engaged with Miss Frederick in the fantasy classified 'FM1,' which, by its description, I take to designate 'farm number one.'"

"There's a series?" Mr. Dunn asked.

"There are a lot of different animals on a farm," Mr. Lightner said.

"And just how familiar with this particular series are you?" I asked.

"Not very."

"Well, well," Mr. Dunn said, "figure the city marshal for an animal man. Which one?"

"None, actually. He was a milkmaid. The point being that Mrs. Woodley's notes indicated that he used an object on Mr. Dunn with which she was unfamiliar. Its description matches this."

"Did you get a close look at it?" Mr. Dunn asked.

"I didn't have the time."

"There's blood on it. Some stains, anyway."

"It looks like there must have been a fair amount of blood on it."

"Anne cleaned it off," Mr. Lightner said.

"That would make sense," Mr. Dunn said. "Except nobody bothered to patch me up after I got hit. And when I woke up in jail, the back of my head wasn't scabbed over much."

"You don't think the city marshal hit you with this?"

"No reason to doubt Mrs. Woodley's notes. I'm just saying that if Anne had to wipe a lot of blood off this stick, most of it wasn't mine."

"If the stick isn't one of her props," I said, "and it wasn't familiar to Mrs. Woodley ..."

"Then Anne kept it hidden," Mr. Lightner said.

"And since the city marshal knew exactly where to find it when my singing got too rough for the girls, he must've known about it."

"There's something else I found out at Mrs. Woodley's, but, naturally, the house has kept it quiet. The city marshal enhanced his milkmaid's costume with a rather novel accessory."

"So what?" Mr. Lightner asked.

"So, it was a, well, I suppose you might say it was sort of a necklace. Rather more akin to an Elizabethan ruff, from her description."

"Amanda, what was it?"

"A cheese. A papier-mâché cheese. Cheddar, I'm sure."

We decided that Anne's bloodstained keepsake connected to the city marshal's costume, but struggled to reach a consensus as to how that linked to the bloodstained boots and the matching portfolio, let alone what it all said about the poorly patched barn wall and Walter Clarkson's richly preserved corpse. And thus we were too engrossed to hear the key turn in the lock on the cellar door.

Unfortunately, the holder of the key was not Madame's butler.

23

That key sounds like it's jammed. Just my luck – a rusty lock to aggravate my nervous imagination. Well, I don't suppose I should have expected better from an abandoned warehouse.

So how will I make my exit? Or rather, how will my exit be made for me? If my parents and I were working out a final scene, I'd argue for extended swordplay capped by an even more extended collapse in response to the fatal thrust. Can't beat that for a crowd pleaser. My father would undoubtedly agree, barking his commands in French as he shaped my movements. French was the natural language of the blade, he'd say, protestations of the Spanish and Italians to the contrary. I think he used the French more for my mother's sake, theorizing that the language of refinement and diplomacy precluded her from charging us with cheap theatricality. It didn't and she would, and I'd end up dying a short, sharp death so we could all get into bed the sooner for a respectable night's sleep.

The slight nausea in my stomach tells me that this time, my death will be neither short nor sharp. But it will be permanent. As for respectable, I'll have to leave that to those attending my memorial service. Assuming I have one. No, of course Amanda will organize something. Very respectable. Maybe a few of her rockets fired for a salute. And Dr. Thornton? Surely she can count on him to donate one of the larger shoeboxes to put me in for the viewing. Might have to fold me up a bit, but they'll both agree that it's more fitting than the usual pine box. After all, I was the first chief patent clerk.

Am. Am the first chief patent clerk. And if my mechanically inadept killer on the other side of that door ever succeeds in opening the lock, I might find out for how long.

Funny, he's not cursing. Granted, the door's pretty thick, but I should be hearing a few expletives by now. Unless he's a complete sadist, and looking forward to taking his time with me, so he has his nerves under control.

Great. What if he likes to dismember people? Live.

They won't have to fold me into the shoebox.

Now, now, I'm letting my fears get the better of me. But what the hell am I supposed to do? All those death scene rehearsals, and I'm still not prepared for the real thing. And to think that only a year ago I didn't hesitate to help service a cannon in the middle of a battle. Well, I didn't hesitate much. I grabbed the gunpowder. I ran it up to the cannon. After being yelled at. Three times. By a large gunner. A very large gunner. With a very large handspike. Much bigger than my horn.

That was different. To be shot down over the wheel of a six-pounder, that would have been a hero's death. Even if I'd been handspiked by my own side, my family might have argued for a small medal. No one gets a medal for being shot down over a wheel of cheese.

Or axed. Or …

Wait. He's muttering under his breath. Very low, but yes, yes that's definitely muttering. So maybe he's not the axing type after all.

No. It couldn't be. My ears are playing tricks. No, there it is again. Got to be. I know that word all too well from all those times I thrust wide of the mark.

There goes the bolt. And the door. Too bad the hinges aren't as rusty as the lock.

Christ Jesus!

Father was right. French is the natural language of the blade.

24

"Well, now. A party in my wine cellar, and I was not invited."

Madame Serurier did not look amused. In fact, the color in her cheeks matched the scarlet of her riding habit, and she hadn't yet caught her breath.

"Did you have a pleasant ride, Madame?" I asked.

"As pleasant as necessity allows." She walked over to the barrel on which the Bordeaux now rested, and examined the label on the bottle. "Sensible as ever, Mrs. Crofton. Not so expensive as to tread on our hospitality, but not so cheap as to be unsociable."

"I do my best to strike the proper balance."

"With the wine, yes. Perhaps not with the houseguests."

"My apologies, Madame," Mr. Lightner said. "I didn't realize that Charlie and I were barred from the ministry. Otherwise, I wouldn't have put Mrs. Crofton in an awkward position."

"Mr. Lightner, in what position you put Mrs. Crofton is between you and her. And neither you nor Mr. Dunn is barred from visiting here. Although you will, I hope, not be offended if I say that I am not overjoyed to see you."

"I can understand that. I was, however, hoping to see you."

"You have some further accusations you would care to make?"

"No, Madame," I said, "but I believe Mr. Lightner does have some urgent filing on his agenda."

"I don't."

"Indeed. No doubt there has been a sudden decrease in American inventiveness. I should think Mrs. Crofton could compensate for that were she not preoccupied with her rescue work."

"Ah, yes," I said, "an explanation is in order."

"My butler has already advised me as to the basic facts."

"I see. Well, the young lady who was taken ill …"

"And although I am sure he did not consider it proper to comment to you, he did tell me that he was surprised that you had a cousin in the United States of whom you had never spoken."

"You know how it is with some families."

"But, of course, blood is thicker, et cetera. Even if the lady worked for Mrs. Woodley."

"Am I missing something here?" Mr. Dunn said whilst I rummaged for a response.

"Only that my butler knows Miss Frederick from his visits. To the house; she was not particularly to his liking."

Mr. Dunn picked up the bottle of Bordeaux, now mostly empty, and walked a few paces away from us. I don't think Madame had intended any slight, but she had reminded him that the democratic ideals of the United States that allowed a butler to mingle with a congressman still didn't apply to him. Whether the similar ideals of revolutionary France still applied to him within the confines of the Seruriers' post-revolutionary outpost wasn't clear.

"So what is the relation, Mrs. Crofton? Did an uncle find himself particularly well entertained in one of the American ports of call?"

"No, Madame, Miss Frederick is not my cousin. I simply thought to make things less awkward for you and your household."

"Very kind, but you need not have troubled yourself. As French diplomats, we are expected to generate a certain amount of gossip. I will see that my butler keeps it to a manageable level. However, if medical services are still of any use, that could be more difficult."

"There is one physician in town that I've never seen at Mrs. Woodley's," Mr. Lightner said.

"That is a most curious suggestion. Why would you want to involve him?"

"Why not? If he can be of some help …"

"Are you sure he would not be of some harm?"

Mr. Lightner didn't respond. I guessed that his certainty about Madame's culpability in Walter Clarkson's murder had been deflected back onto Dr. Thornton. I couldn't respond because of the image that suggested of Dr. Thornton trying to wedge his feet into a pair of ladies' red Moroccan boots.

"Yet from what my butler described," Madame said, "it would seem that all one can really do for Miss Frederick is to ensure that she is kept comfortable and under observation. Is that your intention, Mrs. Crofton?"

"I felt that the ministry would be a better place for it than Mr. Lightner's boardinghouse."

"I agree. This house offers better alternatives for dealing with the problem of disposal, should it arise." To punctuate that, she strode over to the barrel preserving Walter Clarkson and perched herself upon it.

"You weren't planning on hastening that possibility, were you, Madame?" Mr. Lightner asked. I braced my ears for an explosion of screechy French curses. She responded coldly, but calmly.

"You are suggesting that having allowed Miss Frederick sanctuary, I would then neglect her care?"

"You might."

"And for what reason would I do that?"

"Because maybe she knows something about why Walter is in that barrel."

"We already know why. We are the ones who put him there."

"Something about why he was killed. That her current hostess doesn't want known."

I was sure that would detonate Madame, but it didn't.

"If she does, she is not so eager to tell us, no?"

I was about to intervene, but the hard look on Mr. Lightner's face suggested that he wasn't going to back off. If I backed off, I was likely to stay on Madame's good side, which was necessary whether I liked it or not. And if Mr. Lightner dug himself into serious trouble, well, he would have only himself to blame for not following my logic in the first place. I joined Mr. Dunn.

"Why would that be, Madame?" Mr. Lightner said. "Why would a healthy young woman with no signs of disease suddenly stop eating, and then sink into a coma?"

"You are the one who charts his bowels, not I. Your speculation is likely to be more accurate."

"Poison. Does that sound accurate enough?"

"Not really. If there were no signs of disease, then it would not have been bad food. And if Mrs. Woodley had wanted to get rid of her, a simple dismissal would have sufficed. Ah, but my butler tells me that even though Miss Frederick was not to his liking, she was a very popular lady. So perhaps Mrs. Woodley, wanting to dismiss her, but not wanting to incur the wrath of her clientele, did think to administer poison. After all, it is, as they say, the weapon of the woman."

"Mrs. Woodley isn't homicidal."

"You have investigated this?"

"I don't have to."

"Why not? Do you know enough about her background? Simply because a woman has not yet been hanged is no indication she does not deserve it."

"There are other women in Washington City who might resort to poison."

"Another lady in the house? One who was envious of the popularity of Miss Frederick?"

"The other girls liked her well enough."

"You have discussed this at some length with them."

"None of them lack for attention."

"The attention, or lack of it, from a particular man could easily be a motive. I am told that with women who kill, it often is."

Mr. Lightner turned away from Madame Serurier and began to pace. She took advantage of the interval to remove her hat. Mr. Dunn held up the empty Bordeaux bottle and gestured to me for permission to replace it. As the two of us were being ever so good about holding our tongues, I decided Madame owed us and pointed to the appropriate rack of bottles.

"Only one, please, Mr. Dunn," Madame said. "The French government is not overly generous with our expenses, even for necessities."

Mr. Lightner executed another of his theatrical spins to face her. "Who tells you all these things about women and murder? Would it by any chance be the city marshal?"

"No."

"But you do know him."

"Everyone in Washington City knows him, Mr. Lightner. If you mean do we exchange visiting cards, we do not."

"He was Miss Frederick's last customer."

Madame gave me a questioning look. I nodded.

"As I understand it, his visit ended in an unsatisfactory manner," she said.

"Oh, I'm sure he got some satisfaction out of whacking me on the head," Mr. Dunn said.

"Scant compensation for the interruption, Mr. Dunn."

"Maybe he was compensated in other ways," Mr. Lightner said.

"Does Mrs. Woodley give refunds? What an innovative practice. Perhaps the best of American inventiveness is to be found outside the Patent Office."

"I don't think Mrs. Woodley paid him, Madame."

"No?"

"I think you did."

Madame Serurier walked over to Mr. Lightner, looking him straight in the eye.

"Mr. Lightner, my husband would not be able to ignore the idea that another man thinks I pay for services which he is perfectly capable of rendering. Should you wish to meet him for a duel, I will be happy to inform him."

"You paid the city marshal to poison Anne Frederick."

"And how would you possibly prove that?"

"On the night that Charlie interrupted him, he was wearing a cheese."

Mr. Lightner and Madame Serurier continued to lock eyes. No one ventured a word. Mr. Dunn and I passed the new Bordeaux between us. Finally, Madame broke away from Mr. Lightner, and into a laugh.

"Mr. Lightner, I must thank you. You have brightened an unenjoyable morning. Now, I think that Mrs. Crofton and I should discuss how best to tend to Miss Frederick."

"You know what I'm talking about, Madame."

"I know that the city marshal is a man of poor taste in fancy dress. Even before the most ignorant justice of the peace, that would hardly prove me a poisoner."

"He wore the fake cheese to celebrate his involvement in a kidnapping that he expects will fetch him a good amount of cash. You're trying to do business with the man who owns the real cheese, but you're not having much success. So you and the city marshal engineer the kidnapping. Walter Clarkson finds some evidence of this, but poor Walter can't help himself, and boasts about it to Anne Frederick. And for insurance, boasts about that to you when you surprise him here in the back garden. Unfortunately, telling you about Anne doesn't keep you from killing him. You then decide that the best way to silence Anne is to have the city marshal visit her again and slip poison into whatever wine he was obliged to buy for the occasion."

Madame Serurier walked back to Mr. Clarkson's barrel and picked up her hat.

"Your storytelling skills are quite good, Mr. Lightner," she said. "However, even the most fanciful story must unfold within a logical framework." She turned to me. "Lest I sound overly critical, perhaps Mrs. Crofton would be kind enough to point out the slight problem with your story."

Mr. Lightner looked puzzled. His inquisitorial zeal had dulled his analytical abilities.

"Timing," I said. "Mrs. Woodley told you late last Monday night that Anne Frederick had stopped eating. A fatal dose of poison should not have allowed for the luxury of that observation in the absence of more acute symptoms."

"Thank you, Mrs. Crofton," Madame said. "But in case Mr. Lightner is correct about the poison, and I am correct about either Mrs. Woodley or her ladies, I do not think that Miss Frederick should at any point be left alone."

"That would seem prudent, Madame," I said.

"My servants are not unreliable, but they are servants and they are busy. I think it best if you and I are the only ones to watch over her."

I'd been outmaneuvered by the French. This should not have happened to a frigate captain's daughter, but I just couldn't be sure about Madame's intentions.

"Please join me upstairs." She hurried out the door, slamming it behind her.

"That would seem prudent, Madame," Mr. Lightner said, exercising his acting skills in a distinctly unflattering manner.

"Anne Frederick's not my whore," I said, heading up the cellar stairs.

I didn't slam the door. Much as I wished to, it was far superior not to repeat the gesture. And as Mr. Lightner was likely to require bail money sooner than later, I didn't wish to be billed for repairs to the doorframe.

25

"Cass, I don't know about you, but I've got that sense that someone's about to break a bottle over someone's head."

Charlie and I had left the cellar of the French Ministry and were heading down Pennsylvania Avenue towards Mrs. Woodley's to tease out whatever other information we could. From the way passersby were eyeing each other, Pennsylvania Avenue felt like the inside of a tavern in the uncertain moments after a loud exchange of drunken insults. I didn't guess it to be the weather: the sun was still out, the chill wasn't excessive, the wind wasn't shaking leaves off trees. Nor was it yet a full moon. Granted, it was Monday, but something had happened while we were in the cellar that was pushing people beyond first workday grumpiness.

"I know what you mean," I said. "Those two ladies up the road: I was sure one of them was going to wind up with her basket around her neck."

"You hear language like that from two guys scrapping over short rations on a ship late into port, not congressmen's wives back from the fabric shop."

"Yankee matron bumps southern belle. Usually generates no more than a sarcastic apology from the belle."

"Like those gentlemen across the street?"

The angry voices under the knot of top hats blocking each other's way similarly split north/south. Walking sticks were rising off the ground, and I suspected not a few concealed blades.

"Watch it!" Charlie yelled as he pushed me against the wall of the nearest row house. A huge potato sailed past our heads and hit the back of a drayman rolling a barrel towards the group of houses behind us. The drayman footed the barrel and turned in the direction of the vegetable seller's wheelbarrow, parked only a few feet from where we cowered.

"I don't think we should stick around for the next act," I said.

"We're only a couple of blocks from Frenchy's."

"Good a refuge as any."

"And I don't have to wait out back."

Strictly speaking, Frenchy Nordin's is a gentlemen's drinking establishment—Frenchy scrapes the tobacco juice off the wainscotting and sands the splinters from the chairs—but so long as a man pays and doesn't break those chairs, he tends to be pretty liberal with his definition of "gentleman." We kept our heads down for the next two blocks, turned the corner, and gingerly stepped inside. To our surprise, the only person in the place was Frenchy, standing behind his bar, idly polishing tankards in the afternoon light filtering through the window blinds.

"Well, well, Cass Lightner himself," he called out. His tone of voice wasn't his friendliest, but at least it wasn't hostile. Which was good: Frenchy may be short and wiry, but he's a deft hand with the barrel stave he keeps behind the bar. "What'd you do, crawl into one of your shoeboxes and get locked in?"

"Don't worry, Frenchy, I haven't found a new place to drink," I said as Charlie and I walked up to the bar and slung ourselves over two of the stools.

"Trust me, Cass, I ain't worried. On what Dr. Thornton pays you, I'm surprised you can afford anything more than barley water. Just that you're the second of my regulars to disappear over the last week. Beginning to wonder whether I ought to go out and buy a toothbrush."

"Who else is missing?" I asked as innocently as I could.

"Walter Clarkson. You seen him?"

"Not recently. But then, Walter and I aren't exactly great buddies."

"Don't suppose he had too many of them. At least, no one seems to have noticed his absence but me."

"That's probably because you're one of the few people he cared to pay."

Charlie kicked my leg. "Cares to pay," I said quickly. Both of Frenchy's bushy eyebrows rose at that. I didn't respond, and he shrugged it off.

"Yeah," he said, "Walter's not known for his attention to his accounts."

"Any chance of an ale?" Charlie said.

I fished out a couple of coins and slid them across to Frenchy. "Make it two."

"Cass, glad to see you're still honoring the navy for its attempt to defend Chesapeake Bay last summer," Frenchy said. "Mister Dunn, is it?"

"You got a good memory," Charlie said.

"Goes with the business. You been on a cruise?"

"No. Moved on to other things."

"That so? Yeah, guess I did hear something about those gunboats being busted for firewood. Seems a shame. Way things are going today, the Potomac might need all the patrols it can get."

"Why? What's going on out there?" I asked.

"Let alone in here," Charlie added.

"You boys don't know?"

"Obviously not," I said.

"Spring for a paper now and then, Cass. Joe Gales needs to stay in business much as anyone. Page two, fourth column."

"Is Something Missing?" Charlie read aloud as he peered over my shoulder. "I hope that's not what I think it is."

It was. We read through the article in silence.

> The *Intelligencer* has today been apprised of certain information suggesting that the whereabouts of the GREAT CHEESE, heretofore safely in the knowledge

> of its custodians, may now be unknown. In light of the fact that General J *****n visits Washington City in only three weeks time, can the nation be certain that no conspiracy to mar the celebratory nature of that visit is underway? And if such conspiracy has been undertaken, can the nation be but certain that it must extend to the very halls of CAPITOL HILL itself? With no time remaining to cure another GREAT CHEESE, even in the knowledge that the good ladies of the District, Maryland and Virginia would rise to the crisis and deliver up their milk for the sake of our national hero, what can save the nation from the consequences of gravest insult but REVELATION and EXPOSURE?

I wanted to rip up the paper and curse, but I closed it slowly and laid it on the bar, shaking my head. Charlie gulped some ale. "Suppose that might account for the public staring contests," he said.

"Which, as you can see, ain't been too conducive to friendly drinking," Frenchy said. "The Tennesseans are real touchy. But seeing as how the Vermonters are mumbling about what you can do with extra thick maple syrup and chicken feathers, can't say I blame them. And the others are choosing up sides. Had to bring out the stave more than once in the last couple of hours."

"Frenchy, when was the last time you saw Walter?" I asked.

"Week ago Saturday. Why? You think this news has something to with him?"

"Oh, just wondering out loud, really. You know how keen Walter is to impress Joe Gales. He'd love nothing more than to come up with a story that would cause this kind of commotion."

"Cass, if this was Walter's story, he'd be in here right now bragging about it and running up his tab."

"Maybe not if it was a fake."

Frenchy looked puzzled. Charlie smiled and chimed in. "Yeah, yeah, like a kid pulling a prank. Set that old water bucket on top of the school door and hide in the bushes until the schoolmaster walks over to open it."

"Something like that," I said. "Put yourself in Walter's shoes, Frenchy. Joe Gales keeps sinking your ideas to the point where he's skeptical about anything you have to offer. And then you finally pitch him a load of gunpowder that's too good to resist. If I were Walter, I might want to lay low until I saw how it exploded."

Frenchy scratched at his bald spot. "Maybe. Maybe."

"So do you remember him saying anything that might give us a clue one way or the other?"

"It was a Saturday night, Cass. You know, busy."

"Hey, like I said, I'm just thinking out loud. Curiosity. Only if Walter's tab isn't quite up to date, you might want to know if he's about to get himself into trouble."

"You mean if Joe Gales finds out the story's fake, he'll be prowling around with a shotgun."

"He'd only be defending his reputation as the honest voice of Mr. Madison's administration. I imagine he'd be allowed to fire off a charge or two without official intervention."

"All that buckshot ricocheting off these fine tankards," Charlie said. "Not good for business."

"Nah, Joe's a gentleman. He'd grab Walter by his collar and haul him outside first," Frenchy said. "But let me think. Walter came in early, maybe six, six-thirty. Didn't settle in for the evening, though. Had a beer, then said he was on his way to Mrs. Woodley's."

Charlie shrugged at me. If Walter had indeed gone to Mrs. Woodley's, they hadn't crossed paths.

"Special occasion?" I asked.

"With Walter? Must've been. But I don't recall him saying."

"Could be he came into some unexpected cash," Charlie said.

"Like a payment from Joe Gales," Frenchy said.

"Or even someone else," I said. "Walter may not have dreamed up the story on his own. If it's fake."

"Now you're beginning to sound like the paper," Frenchy said. "Conspiracy this and that."

"No telling who Walter might have mixed himself up with," I said.

"Or who might have him over a barrel. Or vice-versa," Charlie said. I kicked his leg, finished my ale, and declined a refill. Charlie reluctantly did the same.

"No, I think you might be right about the whole thing being a prank," Frenchy said.

"Better for business to spread that word," Charlie said.

"Not Joe Gales' business. Have to be careful about how I sound off."

"Frenchy, if you were more civic minded, you'd be a natural to head a businessmen's association for Washington City," I said.

"I am civic minded. Joe Gales can take some teasing. It's a real pain to clean up a street full of window glass."

Thus confident that Frenchy would do his best to counter the news story and head off the Great Cheese Insurrection of '15, we started for the door and Mrs. Woodley's.

"Hey, Cass! There's another thing you missed last week besides Walter," Frenchy said. "Little odd. Stranger came in soaked clear to his armpits. Not too sweet-smelling, either, and between the two conditions, I asked him to move on. Stared me down until I reached for my stave. Then he got all apologetic, just wanted a whiskey from the famous Frenchy Nordin's. Figured we could stand him at least one shot."

"Hasn't rained in several days,' Charlie said.

"That was my observation," Frenchy said. "He told me he'd been doing some night fishing on Tiber Creek. Lost his footing and decided to pack it in."

"New clerks. Hiring them with less and less sense," I said.

"Wasn't a clerk. Dressed in a hunting shirt. Greasy. Add creek water, worsen smell. And he kept rubbing his arm, like he'd strained it."

"Fish in the creek don't get that big," Charlie said. "This fellow tall and red-haired? Beard?"

"No. Stocky and sandy hair. Hadn't shaved in a while, but no real beard." He snorted a laugh. "Famous Frenchy Nordin's. Maybe I ought to think about opening a second place."

"Could be a whole new business model," I said.

"Get me a patent. Earn you a bottle or two. The good stuff."

"Got any more ideas?" Charlie said. "Or should I whittle myself a pole and start fishing? See if I can replicate the man's actions."

Leaving Frenchy's, we'd eased our way out of the commercial district and started slogging through the thickets along Tiber Creek. The wet stranger wasn't Tom Coleman, but a hunter with a strained arm and an unlikely explanation? Cousin Ray? Worth a look, but nearly an hour's close inspection hadn't turned up more than a few broken cattails. Charlie wanted a rest and I needed a think. Reckoning by the second ransom note, we now had slightly over twenty-four hours to find the cheese, assuming that Frenchy deflected the riot. But what I couldn't fathom was who stood to benefit from provoking that riot before the deadline had passed. My thought was to confront the city marshal and embarrass him into talking, but Charlie and I agreed that the odds against being tossed in a cell weren't in our favor. Charlie's thought was to confront Joe Gales, but the odds of him divulging the source of the story without our using violence seemed lower than staying clear of jail. As I still hoped to stay on the federal payroll, Gales wasn't a good man to turn into an enemy.

"Give me a few more minutes," I said. "I'm not planning on a night in the woods."

"I'm not planning on a night in a hospital tent. We either do something productive before dark, or I'm going to find some branches and set up a safe shelter.."

"Trust Frenchy. His stave commands a lot of agreement."

"I trust him. But all it takes is one guy quick enough to duck and throw some syrup."

"Then maybe the best thing is just to get the boots, go back to the ministry, and see if that doesn't jar Madeleine into a confession."

"I doubt she'll be any more obliging this evening than she was this afternoon. I still think they're safest under your bed until we come up with another piece of hard evidence."

"So we really need to go back to Mrs. Woodley's, get a look at her register, and verify whether or not Walter visited Anne."

"You're on your own in there. Right now, that's not the best strategy."

"I can manage."

"You get your head cracked, I don't want to have to make excuses to Amanda. She's been too nice to me. More to the point, I ain't liable to find another white man to vouch for me on short notice, and if I could, he's liable to take the word 'master' more seriously than you. So the way I see it ..."

"Shh!"

"Okay, if you don't want my advice ..."

"No, listen!"

Faint splashing sounds were coming from further up the creek, followed shortly by faint but unmistakable grunts. More than a few.

"Like I said to Frenchy, nothing swims in this creek big enough to put up that kind of fight," Charlie said.

"Someone trying to free a boat?"

"Not much to snag on."

"Someone drowning?"

"Be pretty far gone if it was."

"We better go see."

We picked our way through the brush as quickly as caution allowed. As we got closer to them, the sounds came at us in a rhythm: grunt-splash, grunt-splash. Stop. Grunt-splash, grunt-splash. Stop. Et cetera.

"God almighty," I whispered. "I don't believe it!"

"Cass, looks like you might keep your job after all."

In the last bits of twilight we saw two men in long dark coats and wide-brimmed hats standing in the creek, hauling on ropes. The edge of a crate broke the surface of the water. Judging from the exertions of the two men, the crate was very large and very weighty. And the edge had been patched with some sort of cloth.

"Canvas?" I said.

"Or maybe oilcloth. Better quick patch if you don't have the time or skills for a proper refit of wood slats."

"And any ship's master would know to do that."

"Sure. Why?"

"Look at the guy on the far rope. He steps differently than his friend when he leans in to haul."

Charlie studied the man for a few more cycles of grunt-splash as the sides of the crate started to emerge. "Yeah, he sure does. Like maybe he's got a limp."

"Not someone you'd draft to haul a huge crate off a creek bed."

"So maybe he's the one in charge, and playing it real close to the vest."

"Less people to talk, and less people to cut in on the money."

"'Bout the way I'd expect old Captain Peterman to work. Which probably would make the other fellow Cousin Ray."

"Which probably would make Tom Coleman dead if he'd found Cousin Ray, or a much better liar than we thought."

"Neither one, Mr. Lightner," said the voice behind us in a familiar deep-baritone country drawl. Unfortunately, two clicks punctuated the statement. As commanded, we turned around with our hands raised and found ourselves facing Tom Coleman's cocked double-barrel shotgun.

"So you found your cousin," I said, trying to stay calm despite the rapid escalation of my heartbeat.

"Yep," Coleman said.

"And had he double-crossed you?"

"I guess you could say that he did."

"But you're a forgiving soul," Charlie said.

"I was raised on the Good Book," Coleman said. "Seemed only Christian to turn the other cheek once he'd said his piece."

"And I don't suppose your share of a rather large amount of money was mentioned," I said.

"There was a few details that Ray'd forgot to mention when we offloaded that cheese into his barn. But he remembered right good by the third time I pulled his head up for air."

Coleman turned us back around and marched us to the spot on the creek bank where Ray and Peterman had just about finished hauling out the crate. They'd shoveled out a path that led a few yards to a small covered wagon hitched to a couple of mules.

"Found these two spyin' on us," Coleman announced as Cousin Ray and Peterman reached a stop in the hauling cycle. Peterman threw down his rope, climbed onto the bank, and limped up to us. He wiped the sweat dripping down into his eyes.

"Damn if it ain't Charlie boy and the government man," Peterman said. "Well, now, Charlie boy, trained with good navy money and still not smart enough to look out for a guard."

"Well, now, Captain, trained as a ship's master and still not smart enough to let the mules do your work."

Peterman took his right fist and slammed Charlie hard in the stomach, doubling him over and landing him on his knees. I took a step towards Peterman, but froze as Coleman put the shotgun to my neck.

"That's right, government man. He ain't worth getting your head blown away for. But maybe still worth something at auction."

"I'll finish you off first, Captain," Charlie grunted.

Peterman picked up the shovel lying in the path and whacked Charlie on the head, sending him to the ground. "Maybe not worth the trouble getting him to the auctioneer." He dropped the shovel, limped back to his rope, and he and Cousin Ray finished hauling the crate onto the path. As best I could tell, Charlie was still breathing.

"Do me a favor, Ray," Peterman said. "Roll that one into the creek."

That was the last I saw of Charlie and the first I saw of Peterman's fist.

26

"Mrs. Crofton, it is past nine a.m. on a Wednesday morning. It is neither Christmas Day nor July fourth. He should be sitting where you are, at his desk."

Dr. Thornton took no great pains to mask his annoyance as he rummaged through the Patent Office shoeboxes. Whatever papers he sought could not be readily found, and the logic of Mr. Lightner's filing system eluded him. Since I believed that Mr. Lightner had taken great pains to ensure that very result in the interests of job security, I was not about to offer any insights that might compromise his efforts, even if I didn't agree with his long-term career plans.

"And I don't mind telling you that I am not pleased with his dereliction of duty regarding these files. I instructed him at the end of last week that reorganization was a priority task. You can see the results of his neglect."

There are people in Washington City who would regard a temporary necessity for the Superintendent of Patents to fetch his own paperwork as a breakdown in the American work ethic, quite possibly meriting investigation by Congressional committee. I'm not one of them.

"Dr. Thornton, my understanding was that your instructions emphasized rethinking the aesthetics of the presentation of the boxes rather than rethinking the placement of their contents. From where

I sit, Mr. Lightner was well on his way to fulfilling those instructions when his efforts were interrupted."

"Whether Mr. Lightner interpreted my instructions correctly or not, the fact is that he remains absent without my approval."

"He must have sent some message."

"When I arrived Monday morning, I found a brief note slipped under the door."

"And?"

"It explained that he would be somewhat delayed in getting to work. In view of Sunday's second ransom note, I might be inclined to approve that. But forty-eight hours lateness fails to meet my definition of 'somewhat.'"

"If he's been pressed into service with the District militia, he might not have had time to send another message."

"Only a small number of horsemen have been called out. Bandsmen aren't of much use in preventing civil disturbance."

"Then I fear he is in some danger."

The look of concern on Dr. Thornton's face suggested that he was not unsympathetic, which, in turn, suggested that I was correct in evaluating his capacity for murder. So perhaps Madeleine was trying to shift our attention away from her, and not just defending her sense of privilege.

"The great cheese is also in danger," Dr. Thornton said. "I believe we're now past the deadline set in that second note."

"To hell with the bloody cheese!"

"Mrs. Crofton!"

"It is probable that Mr. Lightner's life is at stake on account of that cheese, but obviously that is of little concern to you."

"You are very much mistaken. I am responsible for the welfare of both."

"But the cheese is of greater importance."

"To be frank, in political terms, yes. You were just on the streets. You can see how close we are to insurrection."

"That may be your judgment and that of Mr. Gales, but apparently not that of the District Commissioners. Why else would they see fit to call out only a small number of horsemen?"

"Money. Their aim is to forestall trouble at the least possible cost. That doesn't lessen the threat. And if the second note is to be believed, something is about to happen that will turn that threat into a potentially murderous reality."

"That reality has already overtaken an amateur journalist named Walter Clarkson. Should Mr. Lightner end up the same way, I will see you punished for it."

Shock now crossed Dr. Thornton's face, but he managed to keep control of his voice. "I'll excuse that remark as a natural consequence of female distress."

Had his decanter of port been within reach, I'd have swung it. However, I didn't think the rude inkwell on Mr. Lightner's desk would inflict sufficient pain to be worth the replacement paperwork when he returned. I thus decided against an immediate physical response.

"Excuse what you like, Doctor, but since you know that I am not a person given to idle promises, perhaps you should explain what you know about Walter Clarkson's death."

"Has it been reported in the newspapers?"

"Not so far as I'm aware."

"Then why do you think I know anything other than what you've just told me? And more to the point, how do you know about it?"

"In both cases, the answer is Madeleine Serurier."

Dr. Thornton walked to one of the bookcases displaying a number of the office's model inventions. He rotated the barrels of a miniature multiple-barreled artillery piece, straightened the oars of a small steam-propelled flatboat, and smiled.

"You are recalling that ridiculous argument that Madame Serurier and I had at Saturday's Marine Band concert."

"I don't recall either of you thinking it ridiculous at the time."

"My dear Mrs. Crofton, we were arguing about privies."

"You were arguing about injury. Injury leading to death. An indiscreet location for a death doesn't render it less lethal, or an argument about it less serious."

"Are you telling me that Mr. Clarkson was killed in a privy? Is that what I'm supposed to know?"

The question was tendered with a fair amount of incredulity. Dr. Thornton suffers from the occasional urge for melodramatics, but I was pretty sure this wasn't one of those occasions.

"Walter Clarkson was found a week ago Monday with the back of his head bashed in. The position of his body indicated that when bashed, he had been on his way out of the privy in the back garden of the French Ministry."

"Good God! That's why she started the argument."

"In fact, Madame Serurier may have thought I'd started the discussion as a signal to her. I didn't."

"Who found the body?"

"One of Madame's footmen. Mr. Lightner was dining with me at the ministry, so when her butler reported the footman's discovery, Madame and the two of us went to investigate." As Dr. Thornton had plenty on which to ruminate, I thought it best to leave any potential jealousies from the mention of Charlie Dunn's presence untriggered.

"Does Louis Serurier know about this?"

"I believe Madame and the ministry staff have done their best to maintain his ignorance."

"I gather that the city marshal and the police constables are also unaware of the death."

"Certainly the constables. The marshal might be aware, but not by way of any official report."

Dr. Thornton went to the window and stared out. "You know that Madeleine and I often argue on a wide range of topics," he said.

"The process does seem to keep her amused."

"I suppose it amuses me as well. But we don't push each other to the point of genuine irritation, or if we do, it's not done in public. So to test me like she did at the concert … how on earth could she possibly think I was involved in a murder?"

I didn't want to tell him that his chief clerk thought the same thing. "I honestly couldn't say. But I can tell you that Walter Clarkson positioned himself in the alley behind your office on the day you instructed Mr. Lightner about the cheese-napping. He overheard enough of your conversation to pursue the matter further."

Dr. Thornton quickly shut the window. "And did she know that when you found the body?"

"We may have alluded to it whilst evaluating the situation."

"And how did you ultimately evaluate it? Where is Mr. Clarkson now?"

27

"Good morning, Mr. Lightner. I hope I did not rouse you too early, but it is already well past nine."

"No, no, I've been up for hours. Didn't want to miss the little shafts of sun peeking through the rotten shutters."

"I am glad to see that you have maintained your wits. These are not the most salubrious of accommodations."

"I've stayed in worse. Except for the chain."

Madame Serurier knelt beside me, pushed back the hood of her cloak, and touched my face. When I flinched, her apology was genuine enough to keep me from reaching for her neck.

"Captain Peterman is a *couchon.* He did not even tell me you were here until late yesterday."

"You know the old saying about lying down with pigs. Maybe you should have employed someone else."

"Maybe. He was the least objectionable choice."

"Did he tell you what he did with Charlie?"

"The issue has been addressed."

"Did he tell you he killed him?"

"Shortly after you were brought here, Mr. Coleman and his cousin were ordered back to Tiber Creek."

"Not by Peterman."

"No. At any rate, Mr. Dunn had vanished. In light of the weak current, that would suggest his survival."

"Or he could be lying on a table in some doctor's cellar, waiting to be dissected."

She frowned at me, then took a handkerchief and a small jar from her reticule and dabbed at the bruises above my jaw. Between the cool mint of the ointment and the warm vanilla of her perfume, I almost felt comforted.

"I am afraid I do not have a steak to reduce the swelling of your eye."

"Can't expect you to have thought of everything." I had to admit, the fact that she thought to bring the ointment suggested that the purpose of her visit wasn't murder. Unless this was some sort of bizarre French death ritual.

She cushioned my head against her breasts and examined the other side of my face. If she were about to cut my throat, I didn't care.

"Aside from your face, it appears that the captain was lenient with you," she said.

"I don't think he broke anything. You're welcome to double check."

She put away the ointment and eased herself onto her feet. "I shall leave that privilege for Mrs. Crofton." But instead of unlocking my chain, she walked slowly around the cheese, sniffing at it, caressing it.

"It does not appear to be a bad effort," she said.

"Worth killing for?"

"Mr. Lightner, once and for all, I have not killed anyone, nor have I ordered anyone else to do so. I misled you about the pertinence of my acquaintance with Samuel Brackenridge, and as to my knowledge of the whereabouts of the cheese. Despite some risk to the city, I provided the *National Intelligencer* with volatile information so that the cheese could be safely removed from Tiber Creek during the ensuing distraction. Otherwise, I have conducted my business as a lady. And I am not your enemy."

"Then as a friend, would you mind releasing me?"

"I am afraid I am not able to do that."

"Of course. You can't bring yourself to kill a friend, so you're going to let Peterman finish me off. But you'll be kind enough to let Amanda visit first."

"Mr. Lightner, I do not have the key."

Another woman with a talent for picking locks. She and Amanda could start a burglary ring.

"Don't tell me this whole thing was Peterman's idea."

"Certainly not! He acts solely as my servant."

"And like any good lackey, carries the keys for the mistress."

"A set for me would have been redundant."

"Less implicating, anyway."

She sat herself atop the cheese, resting her feet on the edge of the wooden wheel on which the cheese rested, and to which I was tethered.

"Not a trace of kashkaval," she said as she examined the cheese knife. "Your willpower is impressive. I trust this will compensate." She took a cloth from her reticule and opened it to reveal some bread and a couple of chicken legs. I still wasn't sure that it wasn't my last meal, but I accepted.

"So do you now understand that you have not been kept in these conditions on my instructions?" she said.

"Peterman isn't the sort to leave a cheese knife."

"I do not imagine that he would leave one of this quality, no. But, then, neither would I."

"Too good for a humble clerk."

"Too English. There are French cutlers whose qualities of design I prefer."

"Dr. Thornton likes English design."

"So he does. But he was not involved in bringing the cheese here."

"Who else, then?"

"To be honest, I am not sure who left the knife. It was not a detail about which I was informed. However, by process of elimination, I would have to guess that it was Mr. John C. Randolph."

Well, I wasn't crazy after all. He was part of the scheme. Not the mastermind, though. It didn't make sense that she'd be working for him.

"You look puzzled," Madame said. "I take it he is not a familiar name."

"We've met. The future of my inkwell rests in his hands. But surely any concerns you or Minister Serurier have with the Treasury Department are of a more elevated nature."

"As I told you, the French government is not overly generous with our expenses. Cultivating alternate sources is only prudent."

"And as a low-level assistant, John C. Randolph's price is also prudent."

"He admires diplomats. Who better to admire than the wife of the French Minister? In such a situation, even a few handkerchiefs provide a good rate of exchange."

His handkerchief. It was fine lace, not just shopworn. Now, Madeleine Serurier was nothing if not confident of her allure, but in Randolph's case? I suppose if he liked both sexes ... No. Simple bribery. That's all.

"So what's his role in all this?"

"I asked him to make certain arrangements regarding the transportation and storage of the cheese."

"On whose authority?"

"The French government, of course. I told him we had been enlisted under the utmost secrecy to provide special protection for Samuel Brackenridge."

"Which involved moving the cheese from the barn without his knowledge."

"Mr. Randolph had no problem with the concept, except perhaps with the timing. I could not risk taking him into my confidence until the last moment, so his choices in personnel were limited. And as he had already arranged for the initial transport with Mr. Coleman, I thought our best option was to have Cousin Raymond take over once the cheese had been delivered to his barn. He then enlisted the assistance of Captain Peterman. Unfortunately, Captain Peterman decided that the business was too lucrative to leave in charge of Cousin Raymond."

"Just our luck. Cousin Ray probably wouldn't have hit me as hard, or rolled Charlie into Tiber Creek."

Madame sat in silence while I finished the chicken legs. Whatever else she was, she was a good judge of chefs.

"I told you that Samuel Brackenridge and I had exchanged letters," she said.

"You did."

"They were not of a romantic nature, if that is what you are thinking."

I was thinking that at least she wasn't starting her story with a lie. So far, so good. "With respect to Mr. Brackenridge," I said, "I wouldn't guess him to be to your liking in that department."

"I have not seen him in a number of years. To be fair, when I knew him, the figure he cut was not undistinguished. However, what attracted me more was his sense of enterprise."

"I gather that he always had his eye out for an opportunity to make money."

"It is not something to be ashamed of."

"I'm frequently reminded of that."

"Mrs. Crofton is an astute woman. You should respect her advice in these matters."

"As you did with Samuel Brackenridge."

"It was rather I who often gave the advice. In a ladylike way, of course."

"Naturally." And it probably hadn't taken Brackenridge long to entrust Madame with those personal thoughts audible only when she leaned in closely.

"In fact, as far as I was concerned, we developed an understanding that I would be included in his future business plans."

"I imagine that was quite an exciting prospect."

"I am practical woman, Mr. Lightner, and I am cautious about taking too much excitement in the absence of contractual documents. But after Mr. Brackenridge returned to Vermont, we maintained a correspondence. I believe at that time he was involving himself in the wool trade. I recall advising him about his sheep. I do not care particularly for sheep, but business is business. Unfortunately, the war disrupted our correspondence for a long while. Then earlier this year, I began to receive his letters again."

"He asked you for advice about cheese?"

"Who better to ask than a French woman?"

"Did he forward his thoughts about industrial cheese-making?"

"No, he did not." The annoyance in her voice said woman scorned, just as I'd thought.

"Then you found out about the great cheese like everyone else, from the newspapers."

"Yes, as I had to learn from Dr. Thornton about the Brackenridge patent application for a new cheese press."

That didn't necessarily implicate the boss—patent confidentiality is subject to his interpretation, especially where Madame is concerned. But it didn't dampen my suspicions about him, either.

"So I was right," I said. "Should Brackenridge succeed in building his empire of cheese, you want your percentage."

"Oh, more than that. I should be a partner."

"And not a silent one."

"Of course not."

"He's willing to take in investors, but not to surrender control. Thus the cheese-napping."

"I think of it as having borrowed the cheese for purposes of instruction. Samuel Brackenridge needed to be reminded of the more honorable side of his nature."

"I think he'd still see it as a criminal act."

"And you, Mr. Lightner?"

I paused before answering. I could accept Madame's point of view and increase my chances of living, but sensible or not, that somehow rankled the more honorable side of my nature. I could try persuading her to remember the more honorable side of her nature and turn in herself and her accomplices, but I didn't give that high odds. And she still had the cheese knife.

"You and I have at least one ambition in common," she said. "We both seek stability."

"With all respect, Madame, is your marriage in that much trouble?"

She smiled. At least I hadn't hit a nerve.

"Louis Serurier may not be the most attentive of husbands, but I do not doubt the stability of our marriage. The stability of the French government is, however, another matter. Since I was a child, I have survived a slave rebellion, the revolution, the terror, Bonaparte's ascendance, Bonaparte's defeat, Bonaparte's return, Bonaparte's second defeat. And I am not yet thirty. Suppose my next three decades are exposed to as much upheaval as my last three? Sooner or later, skilled in political survival as Louis is, even his luck must run out."

"All right, then, suppose we consider your scheme to be only a sharp business practice."

"I believe Mr. Brackenridge would refer to it as gaining a 'certain advantage.'"

"At any rate, a private transaction. If you could accomplish your goals privately, why send the ransom note to the cabinet?"

"That is an excellent question. I have pondered it myself. But I am afraid I do not have a definitive answer."

"You mean you didn't send the note?"

"I know better than to involve government ministers unless absolutely necessary."

"You didn't send the second note?"

She looked genuinely surprised. "I did not know there was a second note."

"It was sent to Dr. Thornton. Wrapped around a slice of kashkaval."

"When did he get it?"

"This past Sunday."

"The same day we met on Mason's Island."

"And when I presume you were going to tell Brackenridge that you'd borrowed his cheese."

Madame reached into her reticule and pulled out a miniature pistol. And I thought we were still allies. I tensed, waiting for the hit of a miniature lead ball. She then took out a candle, cocked the hammer of the weapon, placed the hammer next to the wick and pulled the trigger. Shower of sparks. Light. Relief.

"I've never actually seen one of those," I said.

"In view of its expense, few people have. I find it more convenient than the usual struggle with the tinderbox." She eased herself onto the floor and used the candle to illuminate the underside of the cheese, inching herself along its circumference in a manner I found very pleasing.

"I do not see any indication of a missing slice."

"You sure? If a slice were removed, and the crack plastered over with some fresh curds …"

"You have watched me take enough exercise," she said as she got up and straightened herself out.

"There's only one person who would have had a second piece of kashkaval," I said, "and who would also know of Dr. Thornton's efforts to rescue the cheese."

Madame laughed. "I should have guessed. In one of his last letters before the war, he complained that Congress was disputing certain of his claims for expenses incurred before he left the Balkans. Quite a large sum, I believe."

I suppose being your own thief does give you a certain advantage. Unless you're trying to outwit the French.

28

"My compliments on your preservation skills, Mrs. Crofton."

"Thank you, Doctor. I'll send you a crock of my marmalade when I next see a proper shipment of oranges in the Central Market. Though I should note that in this case, the handiwork was not solely mine."

"Madeline Serurier never ceases to surprise me with her hidden talents."

I would have loved to have explored that observation further, but with Dr. Thornton up to his elbows in the whiskey solution bathing Walter Clarkson's corpse, I didn't think the time wholly appropriate.

"I concur in your evaluation of the probable cause of death," Dr. Thornton said as he rotated Clarkson's head forward, then sideways to examine the wound. Huzzah. The doctor had weighed in. It was official.

Bloody male condescension. As if I couldn't understand the basics of blunt trauma.

"Now, as to the time of death," Dr. Thornton said, "what were your observations during your initial inspection of the body?"

I'd assumed that Walter Clarkson had been freshly killed when we'd found him. Had I missed something?

"Well, it was nearly a new moon that night," I said. "And as such, it is, of course, quite difficult to make detailed observations in simple lantern light."

"Understood. The basics, however, are the basics. Any signs of the onset of rigor mortis?"

"Not that I recall."

"Onset isn't usually seen first in the stiffening of the limbs, as most people imagine. More typically, you might have noticed rigidity in the eyelids, or the smaller muscles of the face."

I knew that. Why hadn't we done a closer inspection?

"If you had seen such indications, we might have been able to say that our victim was killed within three or four hours of discovery."

It was Mr. Lightner's fault. I'd been hastened by his squeamishness.

"The night was chilly. That might have prevented rigor from setting in at all," I said.

"True. Had the body cooled by time of discovery?"

"Not totally. But then, despite the chill of the evening, Mr. Clarkson's clothing would have provided a measure of insulation."

"Also true. So we should look for signs of livor mortis, otherwise referred to as post-mortem hypostasis. Are you familiar with that concept?"

"Gravitational movement of the blood once circulation has ceased. That is to say, blood in the body will tend to flow downward. Otherwise known simply as lividity."

"Very good, Mrs. Crofton. Madeleine never ceases to surprise me with her talents, and you never cease to surprise me with the breadth of your knowledge." The compliment was real, albeit grudging, but I was beginning to lose my patience with playing careless medical student.

"If the body had been lying on its back," he continued, "you should have seen the characteristic purple mottling of the skin on the earlobes, or under the fingernails. Obviously it wasn't, and you didn't. But then, do I understand correctly that you failed to perform a detailed examination of the torso?"

"Madame Serurier and I felt it most prudent to get the body into its preservational fluid as quickly as possible."

"No doubt that also explains your reluctance to undress the body before immersion. It's as well that your ambitions do not run in the direction of becoming the District's coroner. Now, if you will assist me, I'll take a look at the chest and upper limbs."

I supported Walter Clarkson's arms as Dr. Thornton pried apart the alcohol-logged coat, waistcoat, and shirt. I contemplated tipping the doctor's head into the barrel, but didn't think I could get enough leverage on him. I resolved to take more exercise in future.

"Now, there is some light mottling on the chest," Dr. Thornton said. "As you may be aware, livor mortis would have begun anywhere from one-half hour to two hours after death, and developed fully within twelve. Moving the body, of course, would have affected the process. How did you transport it from the back garden?"

"We used the gardener's wheelbarrow."

"Did you place the body face up or face down?"

"Face down seemed undignified."

Dr. Thornton looked again at the back of Walter Clarkson's head. "Well, I don't suppose contamination by foreign matter from the wheelbarrow is an issue at this point."

"We are only dealing with one garden."

"Accepting your theory as to lack of signs of rigor, I don't think the extent of the mottling on the chest supports a twelve-hour period from death until the body was turned over into the wheelbarrow. Also, you found the body shortly after nine."

"That was when the footman found him upon making a trip to the privy."

"Exactly. I find it hard to believe that an entire day transpired without any member of the Serurier household needing the privy. So let us observe the condition of the back." We bent Walter Clarkson forward and wrestled his clothing up under his arms. "Ah. More extensive discoloration, particularly around the lower vertebrae."

"Then what is your opinion as to the time of the killing?"

Dr. Thornton took his hands out of the whiskey solution and, in the absence of anything resembling a towel, shook them as dry as possible before refastening his sleeves and putting on his coat. I took the sequence as permission to wrestle Walter Clarkson's clothing back into a decent position, lower his head back under the solution and replace the lid of the barrel.

"The mottling on the chest indicates that the body had been lying face down for not much longer than a couple of hours before you turned him over," Dr. Thornton answered. "I take it you didn't leave him face up in the wheelbarrow for very long."

"It did take some time to fill the barrel. I believe it was somewhat shy of an hour from privy to interment."

"Very well. The mottling on the back would be consistent with his having spent the remaining hours until maximum lividity in the crouching position inside the barrel."

"The sum of which points to time of death after six-thirty."

"By which time —to answer Madeleine's ludicrous suspicions—I was already at home with Mrs. Thornton, entertaining members of the House Subcommittee for Internal Improvements."

I didn't immediately voice acceptance of that statement.

"We discussed the office's current caseload of applications for new methods of surfacing roads," he added. "Also our caseload of applications for new wagon tires should the first caseload of applications prove wanting."

I must have looked more suspicious than I intended.

"Their attendance can be verified," he snapped.

"Oh, I don't doubt it. And so long as we're speculating, I don't think that Madame Serurier argued with you at the concert in order to deflect suspicion that she killed Walter Clarkson herself. By six-thirty on the evening of the murder, she and I were evaluating options for supper, and she didn't leave the house until we went to examine the body."

"But you still think that the murder is connected with the kidnapping of the great cheese."

"I'm convinced Mr. Clarkson was killed whilst snooping for evidence about it."

"Which he thought he'd find in the Seruriers' privy?"

"As I understand it, he was not a man averse to rummaging in rubbish. However, it's more likely that he was merely caught short on his way to a concealment beneath the ministry dining room windows."

"In either case, you're suggesting that Clarkson thought that the Seruriers were involved in the kidnapping."

"At least that one of them knew something."

Dr. Thornton sank onto Walter Clarkson's barrel then realized where he'd sat and jumped back up. He chose to pace instead.

"Do you understand the potential implications here?" he asked. I assumed the question to be rhetorical, and didn't answer. "War with France. General Jackson will demand no less!"

I perceived that Dr. Thornton was about to embark on another analytical adventure that had a good chance of propelling him onto a swift horse and down the road towards President Madison's western Virginia estate. Like it or not, I needed him here, and had to reel him back. I tamped down my instinct to ridicule him to his senses.

"Doctor, if another conflict is on the horizon, protocol first requires a demand for redress of grievances. Even if the secretary of state acts within the fortnight, that paperwork will need at least six additional weeks to reach Paris, and depending on the French government's holiday calendar, perhaps more than that to secure an answer. If Mr. Lightner is endangered, he will not be able to wait that long for you to turn your attention to his rescue."

Dr. Thornton stopped pacing and appeared to consider my argument.

"And whatever predicament Mr. Lightner is in," I said, "surely it must be because he was getting closer to the cheese. Find him first, and then we should know whether or not to prepare our frigates to blockade Calais."

"Yes, yes, it does make sense. Of course it does. Do you have any idea where to look?"

Unfortunately, I hadn't been able to slip past Madame's servants long enough to attempt to pick the locks on the doors to the Seruriers' private chambers. But there was one other person in the house who might provide a clue. It was time to see if Dr. Thornton had any ideas on how to get her to talk.

29

Found him.

Okay, that wasn't the hard part. Only a few taverns in the District where a man like Peterman does business, few more in Georgetown. Hard part was holding off jumping him as he staggered out of one in the dark, and cutting his throat.

Figure I owe Cass more than that. And since Peterman figures me dead, he ain't looking over his shoulder, so I still got the element of surprise.

'Course, it ain't quite a half-moon yet. In the right shadows, I might just look white enough to him so he thinks he's seeing a ghost, keel over in fright, save me the trouble of cleaning blood off my shirt.

Whichever way he goes, it's what he gets for being careless. Old sailor like Peterman ought to know something about creeks. Ought to know that even a creek as sluggish as Tiber Creek's got some current. Got enough to snag a man's legs on some tree roots, enough to turn his body and push his nose above water.

Hell, he knew. He stood in it. He was just too intent on beating the crap out of us to remember.

So however I kill him, it's his doing.

30

"Opium poisoning. Most likely an overdose of laudanum." The look on my face must have registered with Dr. Thornton as incomprehension, as he quickly provided details in his most professorial manner.

"Miss Frederick's breathing is slow and shallow, her pulse small and irregular, her skin flushed, her pupils strongly contracted."

"Yes, I do understand. I am familiar with the use of the drug and the dangers from its misuse."

"That being the case, you might have recognized these symptoms when you brought her here."

"Forty-nine hours ago, they were not as advanced."

"But you were unable to rouse her."

"At one point, she almost roused herself and spoke. However, in the absence of a complete personal history, I did not think it appropriate to apply either excessive noise or force to hasten the natural process. If her heart muscle harbors a weakness, the resultant shock might have proved instantly fatal."

"She survived a carriage ride."

"The jolting was rhythmic. Perhaps she found it soothing."

Dr. Thornton harrumphed at me and walked around the foot of my bed to the chair where I had seated myself during his examination.

He lowered his voice. "Luckily, she does not yet exhibit signs that she has slipped into irreversible coma."

"I had noticed this morning that her skin was still warm and dry, and that there was no lividity on her lips or ears. Otherwise, I would not have risked venturing out."

"Mrs. Crofton, considerable though your knowledge may be, your disinclination to seek professional medical advice two days ago may well have cost this woman her life!"

I took the chastisement without contradiction. It wasn't that I agreed—professional medical advice is not one of the better bargains of the modern world. It was perhaps that I felt some guilt over my darker impulses towards Anne Frederick. "What is your advice now, Doctor?"

A hard kick to the shin shattered my sleep, and it didn't come from a woman's boot.

"Get up, Lightner. Time to move." I'd have considered that good news, except Captain Peterman's voice didn't sound any friendlier than Cousin Ray's shotgun looked. I shook my head in an attempt to clear it and struggled onto my feet.

"Any particular place you'd like me to go?" I said. Peterman gave me a hard look. I braced myself for a punch.

"How about that, Ray," he said, smiling. "Man's locked down here for almost three days without what you'd call adequate comforts, but he still got his sense of humor."

Ray mumbled something that sounded affirmative, punctuated by a spit of chaw. Peterman grabbed my chin and twisted my face up into the shafts of light that had begun to recede towards the shutters. "Looks like he's managed to clean himself up, too. Now, I know where you got the water, but there wasn't any mint-smelling grease around when we left. That little slicked-up Virginia boy been back?"

"Nobody fitting that description," I said. Peterman let go of my chin.

"Then it must have been the French bitch."

So there'd already been a falling out amongst thieves.

"What happened, Captain? Did you and Madame Serurier have a dispute over fees?"

Peterman smiled again. I seemed to be amusing him a lot more than I intended. Maybe a few Falstaff speeches would stall the new threat to my life.

"Not yet," he said.

"Almost. Almost. Come on, Anne! Come on! Swallow!"

She gagged, spewing hot coffee over the lip of the cup. My face, dress, and bed linen received an equal measure.

"Slight, but another response," Dr. Thornton said. "Try again."

Same result. I put down the cup and wiped my face. Dr. Thornton shifted Anne's head to his other shoulder and re-braced himself against her back, pushing her torso a bit farther forward. That may have decreased his potential for muscle cramp, but failed to make my next attempt with the cup more successful.

"Are you sure you don't want to send one of the servants to procure a baby bottle?" I asked.

"Time, Mrs. Crofton, time! As she is still unable to vomit up the opium, we must get the coffee into her system as fast as possible."

"I'm well aware of that, Doctor. Surely the spout of the coffeepot ..."

"Without drowning her. The gag reflex is promising, but doesn't assure me that her ability to cough remains unimpaired should her reaction shift the spout and send coffee into her lungs."

"Then it would appear that our next best course of action is the coffee enema."

Anne groaned at that, but we judged it too weak to constitute a protest.

I'd been moved. Only a few feet, to be sure, and my hands were still manacled together, but I was free of the great cheese. Theoretically, I could make a run for it. As a practical matter, I might manage that only if Peterman dozed off and let the shotgun slip from his lap. The constant tapping of Cousin Ray's mallet made that unlikely.

"You are taking your damn time, Ray," Peterman growled, checking his pocket watch. "We got less than two hours daylight left. I want that thing packed and ready to go before your cousin pulls up his wagon."

Cousin Ray nodded, and continued his methodical assembly of what had been the crate for the cheese. With everything else running through my head in the last couple of days, I hadn't really bothered myself about why the crate was missing until Cousin Ray brought in the pile of staves.

"Man fancies himself a craftsman," Peterman said to me. For someone intent on revenge, he was being remarkably sociable. "If I'd let him patch the hole in his barn wall, we'd still be there."

"In all fairness," I said, "if you're going to get the kind of money you want from Madame Serurier, the crate has to be as protective as possible."

"Damn wood still ain't fully dried out. That's what you get for working with a cheap hauler. Better outfit would've had a fresh crate on hand for emergencies." He rubbed his bad leg and leveled the shotgun at me. "'Course, I wouldn't have had the emergency if you hadn't stumbled into us in the first place."

Yes, it was all my fault. No discovery, no beating and imprisonment. No beating and imprisonment, no severe reprimand from Madame. No reprimand injuring Peterman's pride, no emergency plan to re-steal the cheese, no extra work to strain the captain's leg.

It would have been easier on all of us if Samuel Brackenridge had thought to impress Andrew Jackson with something bite-sized.

Tricky business, the large pewter syringe. Even with a cooperative patient, it's not the most comfortable medical apparatus. And as Dr. Thornton insisted that the coffee was most effective when hot, we were faced with the additional problem of preventing burns. I suggested the method supposedly employed by Edward the Second's killers to insulate the hot poker they'd used, but Dr. Thornton was skeptical of that legend, and, anyway, we had no copper tubing readily to hand. We made do with a contribution from my pot of facial cream.

My dress and bed linen became serious candidates for a bonfire.

But the shock of the enema tipped Anne back into the realm of the barely conscious, and Dr. Thornton and I were able to maneuver her onto her feet. I prepared cold towels as he stumbled her around the room.

"Her respiration appears to be regulating itself," he said, a bit short of breath himself.

"The towels are almost ready. Shall I take over?"

"Are you certain you can support her?"

"She's not a large woman. I'm sure I can manage."

"She's still nearly a dead weight."

And you, I thought, are a desk-bound middle-aged man. I wrung out the last of the towels, then went over and worked myself under Anne's free arm. Dr. Thornton hesitated, then eased out from under her and sat in my chair, catching his breath. I paced Anne steadily in a tidy circle in front of the bed.

"Don't walk too slowly," Dr. Thornton said. "You risk lulling the patient back to sleep."

"I do not wish to risk tiring out before you have had sufficient time to evaluate her condition with proper professional distance."

"I'll get the towels."

Dr. Thornton walked to the basin, duly grasped a towel with each hand, then stood himself at the foot of the bed. As I brought Anne around to pass him, he slapped both sides of her face. She cried out, but uttered nothing further.

"I apologize, Mrs. Crofton. I'm afraid there's no way to avoid your being in the line of fire."

"That's all right, Doctor. I'm sure you've only bruised my nose, not broken it. Feel free to hit Miss Frederick as hard as you deem necessary."

Like the enema, the flogging wasn't easy, but I found it quite therapeutic.

I almost felt sorry for Madame Serurier. She'd gone to a great deal of trouble to buy herself a little security, and all it had gotten her so far was a place on the warehouse floor next to me, with her hands roped behind her back and a gag in her mouth. Peterman might have foregone the gag, but she just couldn't resist spitting in his face when he ordered Cousin Ray to grab hold of her. I could have sworn I saw Cousin Ray back off when she did it, but the look on Peterman's face told him that he might be in for some buckshot if he didn't comply. Madame wasn't any more suicidal than Cousin Ray, and declined further resistance. Peterman hit her hard with the back of his hand anyway.

I almost felt sorry for her, but if she wasn't getting out alive, neither was I, so not too sorry.

Tom Coleman had pulled up in his mule wagon, and he and Cousin Ray were now sweating, grunting and swearing as they inched the crated cheese up the boards they'd laid over the cellar steps. There'd been a rather heated discussion of whether to push with hands or pull with ropes; Peterman ordered them to do both. Coleman, reminding Cousin Ray that it was his wagon, claimed the upper position on the ropes. After the first few inches, it was clear that the cousins weren't finding a steady working rhythm.

"Coleman, you got too much slack in the ropes!" Peterman bellowed. "Ray, don't push till he tightens up!"

Coleman tightened, Cousin Ray pushed. The crate slipped onto Cousin Ray's boots.

"Gonna be here all night at this rate," Peterman said, ignoring Cousin Ray's howls. Coleman managed to lift the edge of the crate. Cousin Ray slunk down against the wall, tugged off his boots, and gingerly examined his toes.

"Ain't our fault," Coleman said.

"The hell it ain't!" Peterman said. "You fools got that crate in here, you can damn well get it out."

"You been shiftin' cargo a long time, ain't you, Captain?" Coleman asked.

"Since you were puking pap onto your mama's apron."

"Well, if it's been that long, no wonder you forgot a thing or two."

"Watch your mouth."

"Like the fact that it takes more muscle to move uphill than down."

Peterman limped a few paces towards Coleman, eyeing him steadily, bluffing through the pain from his leg. Coleman stared him back. Peterman then swung around to Cousin Ray and prodded his toes with the muzzle of the shotgun.

"Anything broke?"

Cousin Ray shook his head. Even in distress, he wasn't the most talkative of men.

"Get your boots on and get to work! Lightner can help you push."

As Peterman jerked me onto my feet and shoved me behind the crate, all I could think of was sheep. Flocks of fluffy, milk-laden sheep. Each one strangled by my own hands.

"I killed him. I killed him. I killed him."

Cryptic or not, they were words, they were Anne's, and after two hours pacing and pummeling, coffee finally down her throat, and the contents of her stomach finally in the basin, they were an achievement. She was sitting up in my chair, breathing steadily, her head cradled against a pillow, her hand clutching mine as I knelt beside her. Dr. Thornton stood next to me, preferring to avoid the pile of soiled linen and towels on the bed.

"Who, Anne? Whom did you kill?" I asked.

"I killed him." Her eyes were wet.

"Was it a man named Walter Clarkson?"

She didn't answer, except to let go of my hand and cover her eyes as she began to sob. Dr. Thornton pulled me aside.

"Perhaps we should send for a constable," he said.

"I think that's the last thing she needs."

"Obviously she's attempting a confession."

"I don't see anything obvious about it. For all we know, she could be referring to her pet spaniel."

"And was it the spaniel that fed her the opium?"

"Doctor, the District constables are not the most enlightened of men. If there is reliable information to be coaxed from Miss Frederick, it is not to be gotten through them."

"The city marshal is a gentleman."

"He is the last person we want here."

"Mrs. Crofton, may I remind you that you have been concealing a murder for well over a week."

"And he may have been doing the same."

"You hinted at that earlier. I really don't think he's that corrupt."

"Right now is not the time to find out."

We looked back at Anne. She continued to sob, and to chant her alleged crime without elaboration.

"She could go on like that for the rest of the night," Dr. Thornton said.

"I know. But I have an idea. There's something in the cellar which might open her up."

Peterman was growing more and more agitated. After another round of sweating, grunting and swearing, we'd still only pushed the cheese about a foot up the stairs, and with six or seven feet to go, the clock was ticking against him. I hadn't been able to attract any attention since I'd been captured, but Coleman's wagon parked outside was potentially a different matter. Peterman wasn't yet sure what to do with me and Madame Serurier, but I was sure that he didn't want to be caught holding her hostage. And the edgier Peterman got, the more his right index finger edged closer to the shotgun triggers.

Coleman, Cousin Ray and I had stopped for a moment to get our wind. Peterman barked at us, waiving the shotgun. Coleman yelled back, and the two began an extended exchange of expletives. Cousin Ray took the opportunity to lean himself against the staircase wall and began to remove his boot.

I glanced over at Madame. Her wrists twisted against the ropes, but they were still held fast.

Now was as good a time as any.

"Anne, look at this. Look!"

Her eyes widened as I held out the whittled tree branch.

"What is it?"

"You shouldn't, you shouldn't have … it's private!"

"I doubt that you'd rather I'd left it at Mrs. Woodley's. Tell me what it is."

She turned her face away before answering. "It … it's a handle."

"I gathered that. A handle for what?"

"A press. A cider press."

So we'd guessed right. I glanced at Dr. Thornton. His eyes had also widened upon hearing this last bit of information. The sketches in his desk! Gears and a platform. A cider press? No, a cheese press based on a cider press, and undoubtedly to be bolstered by paperwork that would show Dr. Thornton to be the prior inventor of

Brackenridge's improvements. His "certain advantage" in getting a piece of Brackenridge's business. But that challenge could wait until I'd finished questioning Anne.

"The bloodstains aren't Walter Clarkson's, are they?"

She didn't answer.

"Are they?"

"No."

"Then whom did you kill?" Dr. Thornton asked.

She started to answer, hesitated. I motioned to Dr. Thornton to stay quiet, and suppressed my urge to break the French mantle clock as it drilled its irregular beat through the silence.

"My father. I killed my father."

"With the handle?" I asked.

"Yes. And then the city marshal took it from me and killed the Italian. And really, it was all President Jefferson's and General Jackson's fault. But I couldn't kill them. So I had to die instead."

It was a decent idea.

With Cousin Ray engrossed in his boot and Peterman and Coleman engrossed in cursing each other out, I struck. I threw the chain connecting my manacles around Cousin Ray's neck, pulled hard, and twisted him around in front of me to face Peterman's shotgun, pinning his arms with my knees. Cousin Ray's distress call cut the curses short, and we all stood silent, save for Cousin Ray's choking noises.

"Let him go, Lightner!" Coleman yelled. So the blood tie counted for something after all. One correct guess.

"Untie Madame Serurier," I said. Coleman took a moment to think, then hopped off the stairs and started towards her. I eased up slightly on Cousin Ray's throat. Peterman swung the shotgun at Coleman.

"Get your ass back up there," Peterman said.

"What you gonna do, Captain?" Coleman said. "Shoot me and Ray both? How you gonna get the damn crate outa here then?"

"Do as I say!" Coleman didn't move. Peterman cocked one of the shotgun hammers. I pulled hard again on my chain.

Coleman stepped slowly towards Madame. Peterman stepped back to maintain his angle of fire on both Coleman and Cousin Ray, but between trying to keep his weight off his bad leg and staring at Coleman, he didn't notice how close he'd gotten to Madame's outstretched legs.

She kicked. Peterman went down, one shotgun barrel went off.

It was a decent idea. Really.

The former President Jefferson and the current General Jackson hadn't killed the occasionally Italian Charlie Dunn, but they had collided in Anne Frederick's mind by way of a giant press. This was her father's cider press, apparently a rather complicated contraption which tended to break handles, and on which he was attempting to create the perfect Spitzenberg apple cider with which to honor Mr. Jefferson.

"As I told Cassius," Anne said, staring past us, her voice flat, "the blend was tricky. My father kept having to adjust the press. The last time he did that, it was taking a long time. The new handle was leaning on a pile of apples. My brother decided to play a batting game. I threw the apples and he batted. Then I wanted to bat. We argued. Girls aren't supposed to bat. I got angry, we tussled, and I got the handle. He threw. Hard as he could. But I hit the apple anyway, and a big chunk went flying at my father. He turned towards us real quick, his mallet slipped, a wedge got knocked loose. We tried to get his arm out of the press. I batted at it, and batted at it, and juice and blood sprayed my apron, my face, my hair. And my father screamed. I'd never heard him scream like that. It took him three days to die."

And thus to Mrs. Woodley's. It was a departure from the usual route of countryside seduction and betrayal, and under different circumstances, I'd listen most sympathetically. But not with a missing fiancé.

"You kept the handle hidden," I said. "How did the city marshal get it?"

"He took it."

"Why did you tell him where it was?"

"I didn't. But I was afraid."

"Of what? Of the scenario?"

"Scenario?" Dr. Thornton asked, apparently not comprehending. So he didn't know everything that went on in Washington City after all.

"Mrs. Woodley's establishment offers special services of a theatrical nature," I said. Before he could ask for clarification, I turned back to Anne. "What frightened you?"

"The cheese."

"Good God!" Dr. Thornton said. "The great cheese has been held in a bordello?"

"No, no, no," Anne said, now somewhat agitated. "The cheese around his neck."

"Papier-mâché," I said to Dr. Thornton. "It was part of a costume. Isn't that right, Anne?"

"It was so odd. And I might have found it funny, but after what Walter had told me, I ... I don't know, I just got very scared."

"You saw Walter Clarkson?"

"Yes."

"That night?"

"Before the city marshal. He didn't visit regular, so, as usual, I asked him if he was celebrating something particular. This time, he said it was kind of a pre-celebration. He'd got hold of a story that was going to make him famous. He told me that he knew General Jackson's cheese was missing, that it had been stolen, that all sorts of important people were part of the plot, maybe even members of the cabinet, maybe even British and French and Spanish diplomats. Especially the French. They're supposed to be our friends, but they're always spying on us, he said. Mr. X and Mr. Y and Mr. Z and all those things that happened when I was an infant. He was talking pretty wild. And when I saw the city marshal with the cheese on his neck, and he started talking about things we could do with it, about wouldn't I like to press my face into it, I thought maybe, maybe he's one of the important men, or maybe he's a spy, and maybe he knows what Walter told me, and maybe he wants to hurt me. And right then, I didn't want to be hurt. So I got out the handle. Only the city marshal thought it was a new part of the scenario, and we tussled over it, and the more I struggled, the more excited he got, and I couldn't stop him, but I wouldn't let go. Then the commotion started over the Italian and I got distracted and the city marshal grabbed the handle and ran downstairs and killed him."

"Did Walter Clarkson tell you anything else?" I asked.

"So you see why I stopped eating. Only that wasn't going to be quick, so I started taking the opium. If I hadn't kept the handle ..."

"Anne, the city marshal didn't kill the Italian fellow."

"He didn't?"

"No. Now tell me if Walter Clarkson said anything else."

She hesitated again, shaking her head in confusion.

"Did Walter Clarkson say anything about being followed?"

"Followed?"

"Yes. Did he mention a constable, or a deputy marshal? A marine?" Well, it was possible. If Walter Clarkson had borrowed sheet music and failed to return it ...

"A clerk. He said something about a clerk. A government clerk he thought he recognized."

"In what department?" Dr. Thornton asked, the tone of his voice verging on incredulous.

"I think ... Treasury."

T**k. Treasury Clerk. Walter Clarkson was either too lazy to block out all the missing letters, or figured that anyone who found the notes he'd ripped out of his notebook would be drawn to the obvious. I found the former explanation more convincing.

Madame Serurier and I were locked in a tight embrace, nestled under blankets, gazing into each other's eyes. I figured Louis Serurier would understand, maybe even Dr. Thornton, but I wasn't exactly sure how I was going to explain it to Amanda.

Hopefully, she'd accept the fact that the chain, ropes and gags took all the fun out of it.

Unfortunately for us, Captain Peterman still had his sea legs, and he was able to recover from Madame's assault before I could let go of Cousin Ray and jump him. With one loaded shotgun barrel left, and to my surprise, an advance of a few dollars, he persuaded the cousins to finish their work. However, he'd declined to give either me or Madame any second chances, and, looping my manacle chain around her back, bundled us together like a pair of Turkey carpets. And like a pair of carpets, we were now lying in the bed of Tom Coleman's wagon, wedged next to the crate of kashkaval, awaiting delivery to an unknown destination.

As best I could make out from the muffled conversation between Peterman and Coleman, that destination was somewhere in the Virginia woods and involved a couple of six-foot deep trenches. In grabbing Cousin Ray, I'd gambled that the French Minister's wife was too risky a person for Peterman to kill. One incorrect guess, although clearly it was her kick that had pushed him over the edge.

Fear was not enhancing my normally charitable nature. Or my hearing. I thought I heard Peterman order Cousin Ray to do something, but I didn't make out what.

The wagon box shifted on its springs. He'd been told to re-check the ropes securing the rear flaps of the wagon top.

No, he was climbing into the wagon. Maybe he'd been told to cut our throats.

He moved slowly. Was he really a killer? If he was supposed to kill us, he was hesitating.

Madame pressed hard as she could against me. I pressed back. We were both shaking now, and sweating.

A hand lifted up the corner of the blanket covering our heads.

"Now how the hell are you going to explain this to Amanda?"

A few moments later, the wagon lurched forward. The other barrel of the shotgun fired, and the mules ran.

Signing Charlie out of jail was one of the best things I'd ever done.

31

It's not that I didn't like my inkwell.

It was functional. It held ink. It didn't wobble too badly. It was just plain. And after a serious beating, three days imprisonment and a narrow escape from premature murder, I felt I was overdue for a replacement. I mean, was a nice piece of crystal and an extra cork too much to ask for saving the nation from potential dismemberment?

In that light, as John C. Randolph might have said, my present inkwell was definitely disproportionate to the status of its user. And I was anxious to hear if he would, indeed, say that, or something to that effect, when he arrived shortly to discuss my emergency correspondence augmenting my original petition for procurement. Or rather, Dr. Thornton's emergency correspondence. The summons, of course, had to come from him, lest Randolph know that something had gone wrong last night with the safekeeping of both me and the cheese.

Well, we didn't know for sure that he didn't. As badly as Charlie wanted to settle scores with Peterman, he'd driven us straight to the French Ministry, where the great kashkaval was now safely ensconced under the genuine protection of the French government. Dr. Thornton had also stepped in to make that emergency request of Louis Serurier, leaving Madame Serurier to work out an acceptable private explanation to justify the cheese's sudden arrival and the curious state in which we arrived with it.

Thus cornered, she wasn't going to warn Randolph, but it was still possible that Peterman or the cousins had. Amanda thought it likely that the cousins were long gone on a hunting trip, and that it would be awhile before they returned to find that the French government had acquired a freight wagon in exchange for its gracious protection of the cheese. I wasn't so sure, but she could be very persuasive in a nightdress.

Charlie had excused himself shortly after delivering us. I'd have asked him to wait until I could help, but I knew well enough not to.

Almost time. I poured two glasses of the Madeira I'd borrowed from Dr. Thornton's office and set them on my desk. A plate of small cakes might have enhanced the hospitality, but the Seruriers' baker was too busy, and besides, Randolph was only an assistant clerk. I didn't want to make him suspicious.

There was a knock at the door. A few minutes early, but at least he wasn't halfway down the Baltimore Road. I sat down and awaited the look of surprise on his face.

The surprise was mine. Two men entered the office. One of them was S. Dunham Walker, purveyor of fine footwear.

"Mr. Lightner?" Walker asked, the surprise now his.

"Mr. Walker. How nice to see you again."

Walker had dandified himself up for the visit, as had the man with him, the two wearing almost identical gold brocade waistcoats and patent leather shoes, and carrying ivory-capped walking sticks. Amanda would have appreciated a peek, but I figured shooing them out would go faster if I left her in place.

"Why, yes, it's a pleasure, of course," Walker said as he approached the desk and shook my hand. He beckoned his companion, who did the same. "May I introduce Mr. Percival, of Philadelphia."

"Mr. Percival."

"Mr. Lightner is a procurement official with the State Department," Walker said. "No doubt he's here to see the superintendent about an important contract. Perhaps some newly invented campaign *accoutrements* for a certain general?" He lowered his voice. "Or a secret weapon?"

I whispered back. "I'm afraid I'm not at liberty to say."

Walker nodded and touched his nose in the classic conspirator's response. "Mr. Percival is a dealer in fine leather goods," he said. "One of my principal suppliers."

Mr. Percival smiled broadly at Mr. Walker. I suspected there was more to the relationship than commercial paper.

"Mr. Percival decided to visit Washington City, well, among other things, to look over my establishment," Walker continued. "He's also something of an inventor."

Just what I needed.

"A tinkerer, really," Percival said. "You know, ideas pop into one's head, demanding one's attention, crying to be midwifed into the rushing rivers of American enterprise."

I knew. I wondered if he knew Samuel Brackenridge.

"Mr. Percival's quite keen to examine the models," Walker said. Percival picked up one of the glasses of Madeira, saluted me with his stick and wandered over to the display shelves. I couldn't stop him without causing more confusion than I wanted to deal with, so I offered the second glass to Walker.

"Oh, excellent!" Walker said after taking a sip. "I must write the superintendent and compliment him on his hospitality."

I checked my pocket watch. Randolph was due any minute.

"Mr. Walker, I think that's a fine idea. Those of us in federal service receive so many letters of complaint that we're often in danger of forgetting upstanding citizens like you who appreciate what we're trying to do for them. In fact, if you were to go home and write immediately, I'm sure Dr. Thornton would be so pleased, he'd … well, he'd …"

"What? What might he do?" Walker was so insistent that I almost blurted something about advising Mrs. Thornton and Madame Serurier to boycott his shop, but I caught myself before incurring a letter of complaint for my own file.

"I'd bet he'd look very favorably upon any future patent applications submitted by Mr. Percival."

Walker's eyes lit up. "Did you hear that, Mr. Percival? Very favorably!"

Percival turned and flashed Walker another smile. "But I'm really only a tinkerer," he said.

"Don't be so modest," Walker said. "I've seen his sketches, Mr. Lightner. They're very imaginative."

"Then you mustn't delay. You never know when the next idea might pop into Mr. Percival's head and demand midwifing." I reached for Walker's elbow to steer him towards the door but drew back, and in that moment of hesitation, Walker's eye found my inkwell.

"You are absolutely correct, Mr. Lightner, absolutely. And since I will be commenting on the performance of a government agency, I'd think that it would be permissible to use government ink and paper, don't you? After all, Mr. Percival and I do pay our fair share of customs duties."

"More than our fair share," Percival said.

You can't argue with a taxpayer. I stepped aside as Walker sat himself at my desk and began to scribble. Percival turned back to the models.

John C. Randolph walked in the door. He was, indeed, surprised to see me.

"You're late, Mr. Randolph," I said. In the normal course of federal business that wouldn't have been a grievous fault, but I figured the circumstances called for a quick attack.

"Yes, I'm sorry. I was preparing additional forms for Dr. Thornton's signature and one of them, the IR – ECCD …"

"That would be Inkwell Replacement – Emergency Correspondence …"

"Cover Document, yes. I noticed that the version in our supply cabinet was the 1813 version, which was created as a wartime document and has been superseded by the peacetime revision created earlier this year. Unfortunately, the department sent this revision back to the printer for correction of certain errors, and it hasn't yet been officially released for inter-agency use. So I …"

"Mr. Randolph, it's good to see you, sir," Walker said.

"Mr. Walker," Randolph said, now as surprised as I was.

Walker flitted over to us. "I take it the items were to your satisfaction," he said to Randolph. He then winked at me. Randolph mumbled his reply.

"Yes. Quite. Very. Very much to my satisfaction."

"A testimonial, Mr. Lightner. A testimonial for your report to a certain gentleman."

"I'll be sure to make a prominent notation, Mr. Walker."

"And Mr. Randolph, now I can see exactly why it had to be those particular items," Walker said. "Mr. Percival, come here and look at this! The Arabian!"

Percival walked over and bent down to look at the portfolio under Randolph's arm. Beads of sweat broke out on Randolph's forehead.

"So it is, Mr. Walker," Percival said. "I told you the pattern would prove most popular."

"You sell these, Mr. Percival?" I said.

"The portfolio? It's a new item, so I'm offering it on a rather exclusive basis."

"I'm sure that's exactly what interests Mr. Lightner," Walker said.

"I need to know if you've made any recent sales," I said.

Randolph glanced towards the door.

"I don't think I should be giving that information to a government official," Percival said.

"Procurement, Mr. Percival, procurement," Walker said.

"Oh. I see, Mr. Walker, yes, indeed," Percival said.

Randolph took a step towards the door. The door to Dr. Thornton's office opened.

"Please don't leave, Mr. Randolph." Amanda held a small pistol at her side.

"My God!" Percival said. "We're being robbed!"

"No, no, Mr. Percival, we're not. The lady is one of Mr. Lightner's agents," Walker said. He then looked at Randolph and gasped. "Oh, dear, Mr. Randolph. Improprieties in the invoices?"

"Something like that," I said. I didn't hesitate when I grabbed Randolph's arm and sat him in the chair in front of my desk. "You were saying, Mr. Percival?"

"Well, um, I did sell one to a rather florid gentleman about a month ago. I'm afraid his name escapes me for the moment. But I remember that he particularly admired the design because of the time he'd spent in the Ottoman Empire."

Randolph pulled the lace handkerchief from his sleeve and dabbed at his face.

"Excuse me, sir," Percival continued, "may one enquire as to where you purchased your portfolio? After all, I am selling on a rather exclusive basis. Or at least, I thought I was."

Randolph looked down and didn't answer.

"You're probably safe, Mr. Percival," I said. "I believe Mr. Randolph's portfolio was actually a gift from the florid gentleman. Am I right, Mr. Randolph?"

Randolph looked up at me, the two salesmen, and Amanda's pistol.

"A gift, yes."

Walker and Percival smiled at Randolph, then each other. Things sailors do on long voyages.

"Gentlemen, I hate to ask," I said, "but if you wouldn't mind coming back at a later time."

"Certainly, certainly," Walker and Percival said, almost in harmony. "Oh, but my letter to the superintendent." Walker added.

"There's a public desk at the post office downstairs," I said, handing Walker the paper. "You can finish there, and they'll deliver as promptly as possible." Which meant a good chance that Dr. Thornton wouldn't see it for weeks. The two saluted us with their sticks and left. Amanda chuckled as I walked to the shoebox stack and got the box into which I'd put the blood-stained Moroccans.

"They are two of the most fashionably synchronized men I have ever seen," she said.

"Did you buy these for Samuel Brackenridge?" I asked Randolph.

"No, I didn't."

"For yourself?"

"No."

"A man named Walter Clarkson was murdered behind the French Ministry. I think the bloodstains on these boots are his."

Randolph looked shocked. "You ... you can't prove that."

"Proof lies in the collective mind of a jury, Mr. Randolph." Spoken like the pompous lawyer I was supposed to become. "Who did you buy them for?"

"I left you the cheese knife. And more water than Captain Peterman thought necessary."

"Juries take that sort of thing into account. Whom did you buy the boots for?"

Randolph didn't answer. Amanda gestured to me, and I poured him some Madeira. He took a sip.

"He was a consul, you know. A very important man. I was privileged to proofread his correspondence. And his plans for a whole new industry! I was so flattered that he wanted my help. But what he asked ... well, the warehouse is Treasury Department property, and even if it isn't currently being used, I didn't have the authority to borrow it. I thought to ask my boss, but Mr. Brackenridge had specifically instructed me about the need for secrecy. Security. The politics involved. You understand."

"I've been thoroughly briefed on the subject."

"So I had to take some time to think. I didn't want to let him down, to let the country down. He kept asking, he sent dispatches all the way from Vermont to New York, and then again when the ship stopped over in Philadelphia. And with the last dispatch came the portfolio. A gesture of trust, of his faith in me. I couldn't refuse then, could I? Especially not when she asked on his behalf as well."

"She?" Amanda asked. "Do you mean Madame Serurier?"

Randolph swallowed a gulp of Madeira.

"When I saw the boots, and the matching pattern to the portfolio, I knew they were the perfect gift for her."

Amanda and I looked at each other. So John C. Randolph and Samuel Brackenridge were strictly business. But John C. Randolph and Madeleine Serurier?

"Were you and Madame Serurier … ?" I asked.

"I had to rush about at the last minute to set everything up. Men I might have made arrangements with just weren't … I'm sorry about Captain Peterman, really. But she said we had to switch haulers so that Mr. Brackenridge wouldn't know where the cheese was ultimately being sent. Extra security, you see. The cheese was so important that perhaps someone would try and kidnap Mr. Brackenridge and make him reveal its hiding place. No one would attempt that with the French Minister's wife. She even had the city marshal on a secret special alert."

A bit of back-up bribery never hurts.

"Mr. Randolph, I don't quite understand," Amanda said. "Didn't you tell Samuel Brackenridge about the warehouse?"

"I didn't, actually. He'd asked if I could find a hiding place, but I wasn't able to answer him before Madame Serurier contacted me. And, of course, there was the problem with the missing key. It's an old property, and the tax foreclosure section, which isn't my section …"

"Had misfiled the key," I said, "and the forms for replacement …"

"Were still at the printer when the cheese arrived, yes."

Hence the odyssey of the cheese from barn to Tiber Creek.

"So when did you give Madame Serurier the boots?" I asked.

"I never gave her the boots."

"You bought them as a gift for her."

"But I never gave them to her! I didn't dare. I come from a very respectable family, and I'm still only an assistant clerk."

"Mr. Randolph," Amanda said, "someone wore those boots behind the French Ministry, and that someone cracked Walter Clarkson's skull with a crutch."

Randolph looked at us with the expression of the proverbial puppy caught chewing the slippers.

"I like women's things," he said. "I feel close to the women I'd like to be with when I wear them. But the boots – well, as you can understand, I couldn't wear them in a place where I could be seen. This time of year, it's quiet in the evening behind the French Ministry. Quiet, dark, private. And it's her garden. But he was there Saturday. I thought he'd seen me, so I left quickly. Sunday being the Sabbath, I didn't return until Monday. And he was there again. And though I don't have big feet, the boots are a bit small for me. I couldn't walk in them gracefully. I couldn't walk in them without making noise. If he hadn't heard me both times, I don't think I'd have hit him."

Even a few handkerchiefs provide a good rate of exchange, she'd said.

Randolph took a small Spanish cigar from his pocket. "She gave me some of these. Do you mind?"

Amanda raised the pistol.

32

"You know, my love, the acoustics in this room are quite well balanced. I wonder if it has something to do with the way sound reverberates around an octagon rather than a square."

"Could be."

"President Madison should consider inaugurating a regular series of winter band concerts here."

"Not a bad idea. It would cost money, though. There are already rumblings in Congress about cutting the Marine Band by half."

"Really? Where did you hear that?"

"Usual channels."

Mr. Lightner gave me one of his all-knowing smiles and sipped his punch. Now that the commemorative speeches were done we were enjoying a pleasant evening, so I decided not to let his smugness irritate me. I could verify the information through my own contacts.

"The cheese is doing a rather brisk business now," I said after sipping my punch.

"No one wants to be seen without a souvenir, even if General Jackson isn't here to see him take it."

"And what do your usual channels say about his Christmas Eve departure? Did he actually take ill, or did he just want to avoid this particular fuss?"

"He's not one to shrink from being honored, and he's not one to crawl into his bed at the first sniffle. My guess is he just couldn't bear the thought of sitting through another recitation of *On Hearing the News of General Jackson's Victory at New Orleans.*"

"And perhaps Samuel Brackenridge sent him an advance copy of his speech on cheese and its place in the American system of manufacture."

"Thanks for not heckling him. I know it wasn't easy for you."

"It's simply that the outcome of the matter still offends my sense of justice, that's all."

"Oh, I don't know. His patent's been refused."

"Anticipated by certain improvements on cider press mechanisms sketched in detail by Dr. William Thornton. Collated from other sources. That really offends my sense of justice."

"Thanks again for agreeing not to confront him. It is a lot easier for us if I remain employed."

I hadn't been entirely philanthropic. When it comes to securing invention rights, Dr. Thornton is still the only game in town, and, like it or not, I will continue to play the game.

"Besides," Mr. Lightner said, "he did go out of his way to stifle questions about Walter's storage and to arrange a proper burial. And to get me my new inkwell."

"You could switch departments."

"Right now, I'd rather not run afoul of the politics. Look at Brackenridge. A Federalist diplomat clamoring for money from a Republican administration, whose frustration prompts him to kidnap his own creation. He's now short of expansion capital with an invention that's easily copied, and a national mania for canal building that's soaking up the investors. No more 'certain advantage.' For what was intended to be a crime without a victim, that's punishment."

"You may feel you can afford to be charitable after the fact. I haven't forgotten that we almost lost you in the process."

He took my hand and gave it a gentle squeeze. We stood hand-in-hand for several minutes, quietly absorbing the music and watching the bejeweled ladies and gentlemen of Washington City swarm around the great kashkaval on its heavily bunted and candlelit platform. For a country without crown jewels, there are worse symbols of national unity.

Madame Serurier approached us.

"The fullness of their sound improves with each performance, no? One may just about imagine that one attends a soiree in, say ..."

"Paris, Madame?" I said.

"I was thinking La Rochelle, or Bourges, one of the provincial centers. But with continued training, next year perhaps Rouen." She smiled at us. "I am sorry I cannot attend their spring concerts."

"Then you've received confirmation?" I asked.

"Unofficially official."

"Have you told Dr. Thornton?" Mr. Lightner asked.

"He and Mrs. Thornton look quite happy this evening. I do not wish to intrude with my business. I will visit the office in the next few days."

"When do you leave?" I asked.

"Not for another month, possibly two. Hopefully by then, we will be informed of our next posting."

"Minister Serurier has performed well here," I said. "That should merit a reward."

"Somehow, I do not think we will be heading for the Court of St. James. You have been very kind in your discretion about *l'affaire fromage*, but amongst the members of my staff, ah, well, who knows what may have slipped into a letter to Paris? In any case, those who remain will be at your disposal until the new minister arrives. I am afraid you will have to negotiate a fresh arrangement with him. Unless, by then, you and Mr. Lightner have negotiated a fresh arrangement for yourselves."

"I will miss you, Madeleine."

"And I will miss you, Amanda. And, of course, the man who did his best to save my life for the second time in less than two years, even if he did almost get me killed in the process."

She kissed Mr. Lightner gently on the cheek. I'm still not exactly sure about the episode in the wagon, but as he continues to show no penchant for restraints, I am doing my best to let it go.

"I think silver-embroidered amethyst velvet suits her particularly well," I said as she walked away to join her husband.

"I think it would suit you equally well," Mr. Lightner said.

"Better," said the voice behind us.

"Where have you been?" Mr. Lightner asked.

"Having a talk with one of the young ladies in the kitchen. She loves my uniform."

"It is colorful, Mr. Dunn," I said.

"It's the plumed hat," he said. "Wins them over every time."

"At least you're official now," Mr. Lightner said. "I can worry less."

"He was worried?" Mr. Dunn said.

"Just do me a favor," Mr. Lightner said. "Stay clear of the Alexandria docks."

"I am a free man, Mr. Chief Clerk. Try not to forget that, okay?"

"I won't."

"Anyway, the new dock boss in Alexandria don't know me."

"Fine. But I think we might continue to exercise caution so long as the whereabouts of the old dock boss remain unknown."

"That's not for want of my efforts."

"Charlie, please think it through. One hanging of a federal employee this winter is enough."

"You telling me that as my supervisor?"

"As your friend."

Mr. Dunn clapped Mr. Lightner on the shoulder. "I'm going to get myself a souvenir. See you in the morning. 'Night, Amanda."

"Goodnight, Mr. Dunn. I look forward to seeing you soon."

The expression on Mr. Lightner's face remained serious as he watched Mr. Dunn walk across the room.

"He's very capable of taking care of himself, let alone us," I said.

"I know. It's just that some people, well, they get an idea in their head, and sometimes you can't talk them off it until it's too late."

I took his hand again. "You couldn't have known. She wouldn't let you."

"Maybe I'll get a note someday."

I should have reminded him that we did keep Anne from dying, that we did our best to talk her past the dark thoughts. To keep her from retreating to another house, or to the streets. But to be honest, I wasn't in the mood to have her ruin my night.

The band launched into *Hail, Columbia.*

"I believe that's the end of the first session," I said. "We could stay for the second, but I suspect our cat's getting rather impatient. He's probably circling the decanter of port even as we speak."

"That's another thing. If John C. Randolph had wandered in the other direction, he'd never have thought to bury the boots behind the office, and we …"

I put my finger to his lips, and removed a pack of playing cards from my reticule. "And I have been very keen to try out Madeleine Serurier's version of whist."

Mr. Lightner recovered his smile.

"So long as you don't wear more than one pair of stockings."

I didn't. And I never will.

CPSIA information can be obtained
at www.ICGtesting.com
Printed in the USA
FSOW02n0912101115
13197FS